Tucker's Fall

Purgatory Masters

E.M. GAYLE

Purgatory Masters: Tucker's Fall
Copyright © January 2013 by E.M. Gayle
Cover Art: Mayhem Cover Creations

All rights reserved.

This book is a work of fiction. While reference might be made to actual historical events or existing locations, the names, characters, places and incidents are either the product of the author's imagination or are used fictitiously, and any resemblance to actual persons, living or dead, business establishments, events, or locales is entirely coincidental.

Tucker's Fall

Purgatory Masters

E.M. Gayle

www.emgayle.com

Acknowledgements

There are many people who go into making each book the best it can be. Editors, cover artists, beta readers, critique partners and very good friends. I owe them all so much.

2012 was a challenging period of adjustment for me and keeping up with the writing wasn't easy. Thanks to the patience and help of Selena Blake, Dahlia Rose, LeighAnna Thomas, Christie Von Ditter, Cat Johnson and my family, I finished the damn book and they helped me make it even better. I feel blessed to have these people at my side.

CHAPTER ONE

Tucker Lewis stared into the crowd and wondered when it would all end. He tightened his grip on the shot of Jameson and brought the glass to his lips. Across the bar and generous play space, fake smoke, dancers in chains, and throngs of half-naked partiers filled the club. The intense edge of the Lords of Acid music and the occasional scream of a submissive from the far side of the room fit right in with his dark mood. For better or worse this was the place he'd needed to be tonight.

The Purgatory club had come to be in a different life for him and the longer he sat here watching the scene around him; the less he believed he belonged. Of course his self-imposed exile hadn't helped much. He'd been riding high on life on borrowed time and didn't even know it. All it took was a simple house fire to bring his world crashing down.

"Wow, as I live and breath. Is that you, Tuck?"

Yanked from his mournful thoughts, Tucker focused on the man standing in front of him. Tall and imposing, he wore black leather that emphasized a gleaming baldhead that drew women of all ages. It didn't surprise him that his old friend from better days and one of the best damn rope riggers on the planet stood there with a smug grin.

"Fuck you, Leo."

"C'mon, Tucker. You know I'm not your type. But maybe this one is." Leo tugged on a leash he'd been holding and a very pretty redhead cautiously stepped out from behind him. Even with her eyes cast down, it didn't take much for Tucker to recognize her nervousness. Her hands intertwined with each other repeatedly as she shifted her weight from foot to foot.

Long, red hair brushed the tops of ample breasts that were barely hidden by a thin, black nightie that stopped before her thighs began. But it was the thick leather collar at her neck, branded with two names that stood out to him.

"I see things have changed for you since I last visited."

"Tends to happen when you disappear from the face of the Earth." Leo clapped his shoulder and took a seat on the bench next to him and his lovely submissive went to her knees on the floor at Leo's feet.

Tucker tried to ignore the slight pang inside him. It had been a long time since a submissive had caught his eye but that didn't mean the desire to have one of his own had completely disappeared.

"Will you introduce me to your lovely?"

Leo beamed. "Katie, say hello to Master Tucker. He's an old friend of mine."

With what looked like some reluctance, the little subbie lifted her head and met his gaze. "Hello, Master Tucker. It is nice to meet you." Immediately her eyes lowered back to the floor.

"You'll have to excuse Katie this evening. She's had a tough time with her commitments lately so Quinn and I have decided to devote this entire week to her correction." Leo stroked his pet's hair and brushed her cheek when she turned toward him.

The pang inside him clamored louder. The affection between Master and submissive was so obvious it was difficult for Tucker not to experience some degree of jealousy, although settling down had never been in his previous plans. "No need to excuse her. I completely understand." Maybe it was time to get back into the scene. He could meet a willing submissive here at the club and work out some of the kinks that had plagued his art this week.

"You thinking about rejoining us? Maybe some play tonight?"

Tucker shrugged, amazed Leo had read his mind. Tucker's body warred with his mind for control. Part of him definitely needed to move on, but the other—well, he wasn't so sure.

"I'd be happy to offer Katie for service tonight. I think it would do her some good. She needs to get her head in the right place for everything she will be put through this week. What do you say?"

Tucker considered the offer while staring at the top of the pretty sub's head. She'd not uttered a word or made a move except for the tiny shudder he'd detected along her shoulder line when Leo offered her services. She impressed him and that wasn't an easy thing to do these days.

He stood from his seat and positioned himself legs apart in front of Katie. Leaning down he cupped her chin and titled her head back until her gaze met his. "I have a feeling I would enjoy your service very much."

She swallowed before a small smile tilted her lips. Whatever trouble she'd been having it was obvious how much she needed whatever Leo wanted to give her.

"It would be my pleasure, Sir."

A part of him really wanted to enjoy Katie. To take part in her discipline and let go of some of the stress he'd endured lately. His self-imposed exile needed to come to an end. He wasn't his father's son anymore. Unfortunately, his body had a mind of its own and wouldn't cooperate like he wanted it to. Flashes of another lovely lady filled his head. A woman he'd not actually laid eyes on in over fifteen years. Maggie Cisco. Professor. Newly single. Closeted submissive.

While he couldn't actually confirm the submissive part yet, his gut told him the truth. She'd been studying BDSM for so long there was no doubt in his mind there was a hidden ache behind her research. And he refused to entertain the alternative of her being a top. That didn't match the Maggie he knew from high school at all. Sure, people changed. He certainly had, but the fundamental core of who you are and what you need on a cellular level doesn't change in adulthood.

He'd bet every last dollar that Maggie possessed the heart of a true submissive, longing to take her place at her Master's side and he'd waited her out long enough. Her reappearance eight weeks ago had sparked more than gossip. Something inside him akin to hunger had unfurled and dug in with razor sharp claws and refused to let go. His recovery had taken a very long time. Too long. Now he needed to rejoin the world, engage in a healthy if somewhat temporary relationship and he'd chosen Maggie to do it with. She didn't know it yet, but he was coming for her.

* * *

Maggie tightened her hands on the steering wheel and held on for dear life. Flakes the size of dollar coins attacked her windshield as she struggled to see the road. Why had she not listened to the news reports when they'd warned the coming storm would be serious? Instead she'd ignored everything around her and stayed at the coffee shop until the roads turned white and her latest chapter had been edited to perfection.

Another chapter in her first book wouldn't do

her much good if she didn't survive the drive home. She narrowed her eyes. Her visibility was shit and she still had several miles to go. Not to mention the hill. A rough groan formed at the back of her throat. Her decision to come to the lake for the winter really had been a very bad idea. As far as she was concerned, Dorothy had it all wrong. No place like home was nothing but bullshit created by some Pollyanna who'd never made a mistake in her life. Small town America held a grudge when one of their own made a spectacle of themselves in the public eye.

Maggie turned the wheel to hold her course on the road and blew out a hard breath. *Focus on the road and worry about your life later, dumbass.*

With her turn coming up, she slowly pressed the brake pedal and turned on her signal. This was it. The hill that stood between her and home. At about ten miles per hour she navigated her small sports car across the road and made her way to Miller road. *So far so good.*

Her car crested the hill and the long descent loomed below her. "Slow and steady," she chanted over and over again. Her teeth ached something fierce from clenching her jaw, but she couldn't stop if she wanted to. Driving in the snow terrified her. It had been years since she'd tried, but it took nothing to recall the tree that had mangled her parent's SUV the last time she'd attempted to drive in the white stuff.

After college she'd moved from North Carolina to Florida where her chance of snow turned to zero and the sun shone almost every day of the year. Not to mention the lack of hills.

Red lights flashed in Maggie's vision and her heart clenched. There were two cars nose to nose in the middle of the road. She slammed on the brake to stop her car and nothing happened. *Shit!* In the back of her mind she vaguely remembered being told to never slam on the brakes in snow or ice because her car would lose traction. In a weird sort of slow motion her car continued to slide slowly down the hill toward the cars blocking her passage.

Maggie's stomach trembled as she pulled the wheel in the opposite direction. Her car swerved to the left, but not enough. As the seconds ticked by and her windshield wipers ushered the snow from her window as quickly as it fell the pit in her stomach grew.

At the first sound of metal scraping against metal, Maggie cried out. The momentum of the hill propelled her vehicle forward bouncing from one vehicle to the other before finally rolling to a stop. With her heart in her throat and her pulse beating wildly, Maggie tipped her head forward and leaned against the steering wheel. Grateful she'd kept her speed low, Maggie undid her seat belt and opened her door. To her surprise, both cars had begun to move and were making an attempt to get the rest of the way down the hill without a care in the world whether she was all right.

She stood in the glow of her headlights, her mouth agape and watched them slide. Slowly but surely, they traversed their path down the hill and eventually their rear red lights winked out of view. Alone in the dark, cold shivered through Maggie. She pulled her sweater tighter and cursed herself for not wearing a heavy jacket when she'd left the cabin. She didn't spend much time outdoors but any idiot knew to be prepared for inclement weather.

Now what?

She glanced back at her car and sighed. Her only option was to go down because on this slick road going back the way she came was out of the question. She hopped back into her car, buckled her seat belt and turned the heater on high. In her rearview mirror headlights approached, making it imperative she get her car out of the way.

Compressing the brake, she put the car in drive and pulled on the wheel. It didn't budge.

"Are you kidding me?" Maggie glanced in the rearview mirror and tried again. The lights were getting closer. When the wheel still wouldn't budge she searched the dashboard for the hazard light switch. She had no idea if the oncoming driver could make out her taillights in the heavy snowfall. Her stomach jumped when she discovered the button with the familiar triangle and flipped it on.

A backwards glance revealed the vehicle closing in with no sign it would stop. Maybe the driver couldn't stop. She'd have to get out and flag them down. She sighed. The car was warm. Out there was not. With no time to figure out another option, she grabbed her backpack and jumped out. She'd barely cleared the car when the vehicle, which she could now identify as a truck, bore down in her direction.

Maggie jumped up and down and waved her hands trying to get the driver's attention. Nothing. He was seconds from slamming into her car. She scrambled across the snow-covered road and across the embankment on the other side. The least she could do was not get splattered.

She covered her eyes and waited for the crash. Unable to resist, she spread her fingers and peeked at the scene in front of her in time to see the truck swerve and miss her precious BMW by mere inches. The driver accelerated and snow flew from under its tires, hitting her in the chest and face like little pellets, as it continued down the hill. Too stunned to move, she watched the taillights move farther away until eventually they disappeared.

So caught up in the rude truck driver, she failed to hear the next vehicle crest the hill.

A horn blasted into the darkness and Maggie screamed before she whirled around to see a large SUV with an emergency light in its window making its way down the hill in her direction.

Oh thank God. Maybe this one would stop. She slumped against the tree and swore if she got home safely she'd never do anything this stupid again.

The vehicle slowed as it approached before coming to a stop at the rear of her car. Bright headlights illuminated the area.

"Anyone hurt?" a male voice boomed.

She shook her head and responded, "No, I don't think so." Her teeth chattered but that was hardly cause for alarm. After she picked up her stomach from the road she turned to the stranger.

"Thank you for stopping."

The man opened his door and unfolded from the interior of the large SUV. Maggie gasped as she craned her neck to take in the sheer size of her rescuer. Dear God, he had to be six and a half feet tall. Not just tall either. He was built like a freaking line backer. His shoulders alone blocked half the light from his headlights as he walked in her direction. She blinked against the glare and swallowed. Her rescuer was as big as a bear and they were alone, on a dark night, on an empty road.

She glanced side to side and confirmed they were indeed alone. An uneasiness she didn't like crawled along her spine. Hadn't she seen this very scene in a movie one time? The heroine had been too stupid to live.

"You're welcome." His voice carried the several feet between them and her heart beat rose. That voice sounded familiar. She twisted her head until the torches most called headlights not spotlights disappeared from her vision.

The imposing figure of her supposed rescuer

morphed into a gorgeous man. Light brown hair neatly trimmed around his head, a strong jaw that lent the man more than a fair share of arrogance and the gorgeous ocean blue eyes she'd been captivated by in high school.

"Goddamn it, Tucker. Is that you? What are you doing here?" The fifteen years since she'd seen him last melted away. She pictured him as he'd been back then. The last time she'd seen him he'd been leaning against the bed of someone's truck with his hands shoved in his pockets and a smirk on his face. She'd been with Derek and far too preoccupied with the outcome of her date to talk to him.

A tight smile formed across his face, bringing her back to the present. "Such language from a lady. Since when can't a man come to the rescue of a damsel in distress?"

"You obviously don't know me very well," she muttered under her breath.

"Whose fault is that? It's been what, ten years or more?"

She shrugged. "Something like that."

"I didn't expect to find you on the side of the road. But I can't say I'm sorry for it."

Maggie's pulse jumped. Tucker looked damned fine and it would be so easy to fall down memory lane… She needed to diffuse this conversation fast. "I'm just glad you're not some crazed stranger looking to chloroform me and tie me up. Amazingly, I am not in the mood for a kidnapping."

Tucker stopped in front of her and locked his gaze with hers. "What makes you so sure I don't have nefarious intentions?"

The steely thread of his comment made Maggie's stomach tumble. Sudden images of Tucker looming over her with her arms bound to a chair filled her head. Her heart beat faster and she surprised them both with a sudden gasp.

"Easy Miss Maggie, I was only kidding. The last time I tied someone up I ended up with a knee to my balls. I'm not looking to repeat that tonight."

The use of her silly high school nickname brought her back down from the clouds and her fantasy land. Although his odd comment threw her for a loop and she had to squelch the impulse to ask what he meant. Not the time. Not her business.

She took a deep breath and trudged over to her car. "You wouldn't happen to have any equipment in that monster vehicle of yours that would tow me home do you?"

She watched Tucker walk to her car, taking in everything she could despite the snow still pouring down on them. Unlike her, he wore a thick winter coat buttoned to his chin that made her curious to know how warm he'd be if she touched him. She shook her head at the ridiculous thought and focused on the situation at hand. *Snow. Car. No way home. Focus.* She needed to get her shit together before she froze to death.

"You staying at your parent's cabin on the

lake?"

She nodded. The less she said the better.

"Unfortunately, this baby isn't set up for towing and last I heard on the scanner it could be hours before the tow truck can make it out here. Looks like you're stuck for the night."

She couldn't read his expression or decide if the innuendo she read in his statement was simply a figment of her imagination. "Figures."

"I can however, help you get her over to the side of the road so no one hits her again. Then you can hop in my vehicle and I can give you a ride home. Once the storm clears I'll make sure someone gets your car out to your place."

More crazy images... Her mind drifted the minute he'd said ride.

She wanted a ride. Oh yes she did.

Why did her mind insist on going there? She hadn't seen or heard from Tucker in ages and even back in high school it hadn't been like that between them. They were friends. Okay mostly acquaintances over the years but there had been moments of friendship. And that one night at the annual St. Mary's Carnival...

They'd been alone for five minutes and they'd shared a kiss. One stupid teenage moment had turned into a lifetime memory she still recalled as vividly as yesterday. His hands tight in her hair, his mouth sliding across hers, taking the kiss she ached to give...

It had only lasted a moment but when her friends had arrived, she'd stood there without saying a word, still stunned by the firm impression of his lips against hers. He'd attempted to see her the next night and she'd blown him off. Now she couldn't recall why. She stared at his ass as he walked around her car. Brain fart maybe?

Running into Tucker like this made her want to flee in the opposite direction. If only to keep from making another mistake. She found him sexy as hell and very tempting. Maggie bit her lip and moved closer to her car. This is what she got for hiding away from people for so long. "What do you want me to do?" she asked.

"Just hop in and put your ignition in drive. I'll take care of the rest." He moved to the back of her car and she did as he asked before waiting for further instructions. Moments later her car began to move as he pushed it from behind. With the steering wheel locked up there wasn't much she could do so she hopped out and added her efforts in keeping the car going in the right direction.

It didn't take long and they had the car well off the road and secured.

"Do you need anything from inside before we go?"

She pointed to the backpack already on her back. "Nope. Got everything I need right here."

He eyed her curiously but obviously decided not to say anything as he turned and headed towards his vehicle. Maggie followed as he led the way to the passenger side and opened the door for her. Kind of shocked that he'd bother, she hopped into the SUV and buckled in. She couldn't help watching him stalk toward the driver's door. His determined stride gave her the sense of a predator going after its prey.

She had hoped to avoid seeing anyone she knew for a while but now that she had there were a million questions running through her brain.

Like what had he been doing since high school? Had he never left home? What about college? What about marriage? Was there a significant other in his life? What if he was gay?

With that thought her own shitty past crashed in on her. If she started questioning Tucker he might do the same to her and she didn't need anyone digging through her closet. Those bodies were too fresh. The ink had barely dried on her divorce papers and the jail cell still gave her nightmares.

She settled into the seat on a sigh. Better to leave high school where it belonged, accept his generous offer to deliver her home safely and then forget all about Tucker Lewis. Yep, returning to her parent's lake home had definitely been a mistake.

Tucker climbed into his seat and started his SUV. Warm air blasted through the vents and Maggie moaned. She held up her frozen hands and ignored the pain of sudden heat across super cold flesh. She desperately needed to thaw out.

"I'm surprised you're out here like that." He turned the knob and more warm air rushed out.

"Like what?" Did he have a problem with her being out here alone? What the hell? She didn't need a chaperone.

"Without a jacket. Or emergency supplies in your car."

Ohh. Feeling incredibly stupid for jumping to the wrong conclusion, Maggie straightened her spine and dropped her hands to her lap.

"What's wrong?" Tucker asked.

Maggie ignored the question for a few seconds and stared out the window. "Why would you think something is wrong?"

"Oh I don't know. I asked a simple question and your whole demeanor changed. I'm not your dad. I wasn't about to start giving you the third degree."

Her dad he certainly was not. She had too much on her plate for the sudden attraction she felt. It made her crazy uncomfortable. Not that she was about to tell him that. She made the mistake of glancing up to find him studying her with those intelligent eyes. The lack of reproach disarmed her.

"It's just been a rough day." She sighed. More like a rough year. "I didn't mean to be rude. I'm more grateful than you can imagine that you came by when you did. I was certain I could make it home without a problem but the snow moved in faster than I expected."

Tucker put the vehicle in reverse and backed up

until he could straighten the wheels on the road. With slow precision he began making his way down the hill.

"These storms tend to do that around here."

After his last comment, the silence stretched between them and Maggie grew nervous. She should say something. Make idle conversation or some other idiotic thing.

Fortunately, Tucker rescued her by speaking up first. "So what brings you back? I thought you were busy being a professor at some fancy college."

Maggie hesitated. *Shit.* Why had she wished for conversation? He'd gone right to the heart of her secrets. "I decided to take some time away from my career to write a book."

He glanced at her. "Oh yeah? What kind of book?"

Uh oh. Here we go. "I've been studying human sexuality for many years now. I figured it was time to start compiling all of my data into something useful."

CHAPTER TWO

Tucker clenched his jaw to maintain control. She'd opened the door with the mention of her studies and he needed to take it slow rather than charge through with guns blazing. He'd known immediately when Maggie had returned. She must have forgotten how fucking insane the small town grapevine was. The minute she'd been spotted at the gas station near her parent's cabin, the phone lines had lit up all over the county. His sister, Nina, owned the small café out there and she lived for gossip. He'd been her third phone call.

That was two months ago and aside from a couple of spottings at the lakeside coffee shop, Maggie had remained in hiding. Not that he blamed her. Curious about her life, he'd looked her up on the internet and gotten more than he bargained for. Fired from her job, divorced from her high profile husband who'd publicly disowned her, and her research discredited. All because she'd been swept up in an FBI raid on a sex club.

The last part had interested him the most. In fact, his interest had soared over the fact they might have more in common than she knew. He'd immediately wanted to know why she'd been in a BDSM club. Fortunately, he already possessed the connections he'd needed to find out. Some quiet inquiries had netted him better information than he'd hoped. Miss Maggie had more than a passing interest in her research. But what did it all mean? He had an idea, although jumping to conclusions at this point was a bit premature.

"Hmm. That certainly sounds promising. What aspect of human sexuality have you chosen to write about?" He couldn't wait to hear the details of her interest from her own lips so he could gauge her reactions.

"Uhmm. Well…"

"Spit it out, Maggie. We aren't teenagers anymore."

She frowned at him. "I'm perfectly aware of that. I just don't know how to start the conversation with someone I've known since high school that I've been studying power dynamics between couples for nearly a decade. It's not usually a topic that makes people comfortable."

Tucker smiled. Perfect. "I'm not most people. And I'm not uncomfortable discussing sexuality one bit."

When she didn't respond, a glance in her direction showed a lovely flush of red creeping up her neck. "Sorry, I didn't mean to embarrass you."

Her hands knotted in her lap. "You didn't. I

just — well — it seems a little surreal to be sitting here talking to you about this. Aren't we supposed to be asking each other little things like what did we do after high school, are we married or do we have kids?"

Tucked laughed. "If you say so. Since your life is making you squirm, why don't we start with mine? Ask me anything."

"I'm not uncomfortable. Maybe I just don't want to know."

Uhh huh. "Fair enough." He dropped the small talk and stared at the road stretched in front of them. The snowfall had not eased and the road coverage got heavier the closer they got to the lake. While keeping an eye on the road, he also watched his passenger. She'd changed since high school quite a bit. She wasn't as skinny as he remembered. She'd filled out in more ways than one. From what he'd been able to tell she'd put on curves in all the right places, especially her hips. God, did he love a round bottom. His cock began to fill, forcing him to shift in search of more room.

Her long brown hair had been cut to well above the shoulders. He was aware enough to recognize the trend but it really worked for her. The hair curled around her pretty face, drawing his gaze to her full pink lips and bright green eyes. There was so much he wanted to know about her, but there was also a lot he'd never forgotten. The last time he'd touched her they'd been too young to understand the spark between them, but they weren't kids anymore.

"Do you think we'll make it? The snow is getting harder and the road looks precarious."

Her questions pulled Tucker from his wayward thoughts and brought his focus back to the road. She was right. Out here it didn't look good. Fortunately his four-wheel drive could handle it.

"Yeah, we're almost there." He continued the trip without conversation. Between his lascivious thoughts and the storm raging outside he had enough on his plate. This wasn't exactly how he'd hoped their reunion would go. He'd been planning for a little more finesse and a whole lot less stress.

The truck hit a hole covered by snow and Maggie bounced with a little scream. In any other situation that scream would have sounded lovely. Particularly if she was underneath him and begging for him to let her come. Instead, she held on to his door with a white-knuckled grip of death and fear written all over her face. Time to distract her.

"I left a couple of years after high school. The situation with my dad got worse after my mom left." Thank God he didn't have to rehash that part of his life. She'd still been here when his mother disappeared and his father had been suspected of foul play. "When my mom returned, my dad turned nutty in ways I can't even begin to explain. The situation escalated to the point that if I didn't leave I was afraid of what I might do."

"Tucker. You can't—"

"I know. His behavior wasn't my fault, but I really hated him. The kind of hate that festers in your gut and if you aren't careful can turn into something really bad. I was afraid I'd end up like him so I took off."

She reached out and stroked his arm. He fought the instinct to shrug off her sympathy. Instead he focused on the feather-light touch of the woman he craved.

"What did you do?" she asked.

"College as far across the state as I could get. I played a little football at first, but after a couple of years it got stale. I came home when my dad died and decided to stay. I guess I was more attached to small towns and family than I thought."

Her hand slipped from his arm and he forced himself not to snatch it back.

"Are you married?"

He shook his head. "Nope. Never married. I did add it to my bucket list though. One day." He winked.

"Wait. You have a bucket list? Aren't you a little young for that? I thought that's what old people did when they started worrying about dying." She smiled at him and some of the heaviness that had begun creeping into their conversation eased.

He shrugged. "I'm a bit goal oriented, so starting a mental list of things I'd like to accomplish kept me on the straight and narrow."

"I can imagine you on the straight, not so sure about the narrow."

"Honey, I'm like a dog with a bone. Once I make up my mind I am determined enough to not let go. Even you're on my list."

Her mouth dropped open. "Why the heck would I be on your list? Hell, anyone's list. That's absurd."

Before he could give her grief for such an asinine statement, a tree branch breaking above the truck caught his attention. He turned the wheel and depressed the gas, missing the strike by inches.

Luckily her driveway appeared and he turned toward the cabin. The sooner they were out of this hairy mess the better. He'd ask her for dinner where they could discuss their lives like normal adults. He pulled as close to the door as the drive allowed and threw the ignition in park. Loathe to let her go, but knowing it was the right thing for now, he jumped from the SUV and rushed around to help her out.

She lost her balance when she stepped out and Tucker grasped her arm to keep her from falling flat on her ass. If anything would make that gorgeous ass sore it would be him not some fucking slippery sidewalk.

"I'm okay. Thank you."

They continued to the door and she quickly unlocked it and proceeded inside. At the threshold she turned back and said, "Do you want to come in?"

"If I come in now, I might not make it back to my place." Not exactly the truth as far as the weather was concerned.

She looked over his shoulder and peered into the snow. "You might not make it back anyway. I don't want to be responsible for anything happening to you."

He was pretty sure he could get home just fine, but he didn't want to leave her anymore than she wanted him to go. Or at least he hoped. He'd been waiting for weeks for her to rejoin the community when she was ready. She'd needed time to recover. Tonight he'd gotten tired of waiting and had been on his way to her cabin. Fortunately or unfortunately, depending on how you looked at it, fate stepped in and offered a helping hand. Who was he to turn it down?

"I'd like to stay."

She stepped back and motioned him in.

This close, he caught scent of her perfume. Fruit and spice that teased his senses. He rather enjoyed that. Tucker glanced around the room, taking in the interior of the cabin. The open space included a comfy living room big enough for Sunday afternoon football parties, a decked out kitchen and a humongous fireplace that could easily warm the entire place.

"Can I offer you something to drink? Maybe a glass of wine?"

"I'm not going to turn down a night cap." He

winked at her.

She walked into the kitchen and he watched her every step of the way. Her gorgeous ass swayed when she moved, making him twitchy to put her on the ground, hands and knees so he could fuck her from behind. He closed his eyes and breathed deep. *Get it together, man. You're supposed to take things slow*.

He'd waited a long time for an interesting woman to come along with similar tastes that might spark his interest again. And the minute he'd read about her foray into BDSM with two men at her side he'd known they had to reconnect.

"You know what?"

He lifted his head and met her gaze. "What?"

"I don't want wine. Hell, I don't even like wine. I want a margarita. After the day I've had, sour wine is just not going to cut it."

Tucker smiled. He preferred beer. "Sure, I can do that." He moved into the kitchen and edged precariously close to Maggie's personal space. "But tequila is quite a bit stronger than wine. You wouldn't be trying to get me drunk so I have to spend the night would you?"

Maggie rolled her eyes. "Assume much? Besides I thought we pretty much already established you couldn't make it back home tonight."

With her hair tucked behind her ears, and the coy smile plastered across her face, she reminded him of the Maggie he remembered from high school. While he thoroughly enjoyed her playfulness, and was eager to coax more from her, he wondered if she realized that all her sass and humor never reached her eyes. Her smile made her prettier than ever, but it was the glimpses of resignation in her gaze that reeled him in. He wanted to peel the layers from Miss Maggie and discover for himself exactly what made her tick. Was she the carefree girl from way back when or the buttoned up professor who spent more time on research than real life? What had Maggie Cisco become and what did she want?

For the first time in quite a while, he was ready to forgo safe ground and delve again into the often turbulent waters of a Dominant and submissive relationship. If she needed a mentor to help with her research, he was willing.

"You're staring at me," she muttered before licking her lips.

"Am I?" Up close he realized her eyes weren't a simple green. There were flecks of gold and brown that reminded him of the freckles on her skin. He took one step closer and watched her eyes shift downward and her teeth bite into her lower lip. He made her nervous but not necessarily frightened. "It's been a long time since we've been this close."

"It has. But—uh—"

Tucker wrapped his arm around her waist and settled his hand at her lower back, leaned forward and pressed a finger to her lips. "Fix the Margaritas, Maggie."

She shivered, obviously affected by his

command. He stilled the desire to pull her hips to his groin. She had no idea how much her reaction turned him on. His balls were tight. He was ready to fuck and they were nowhere near ready for that. Tucker had no intention of settling for a one-night stand. Over the past year he'd dug deep into his desires and decided what he could and couldn't live without. If his hunch was right about Maggie, and he was near certain it was, one night with this woman would not be enough.

Tucker released her and returned to the living room. He liked the open concept of her parent's place. He could relax on the couch while she fixed her girly drinks all while keeping his eye on her. The wide windows across the front of the house provided an excellent view of the lake. He imagined during the summer the area would be breathtaking. A window like that would be perfect to press Maggie against after stripping her nude. And he certainly had a thing for windows.

His dick jerked, forcing him to take another cleansing breath in search of the discipline he prided himself on.

Maybe he should get rid of his boring, memory-riddled acreage and move out here. This place with its cozy spaces and simple amenities was all a far cry from his family estate. When he'd decided to move back home, he'd refused to spend a dime of his father's blood money that he didn't have to. So he'd rebuilt a smaller, modest and more modern place where the main house had stood. His home wasn't palatial, but with his art just catching on he'd paid for it with his money not his father's. Fortunately, during high school he'd spent summers working for contractors to pay for his first car that left him with a lot of working knowledge. So over the years he'd added to the space in his own way with his own hands. That work kept him partially sane. Now that he could afford pretty much whatever he wanted he hadn't bothered. With his home customized to his taste and activities away from the prying public, there wasn't a desire to make a change. Until Maggie showed up.

He caught the sound of her humming behind him and turned back to watch her. Caught up in the task at hand, she failed to notice him studying her. There were so many questions he wanted to ask about her interests. Especially the ones that led her to the BDSM nightclub. Everything he'd heard about her through the old grapevine over the years had painted her as a stuck up bitch professor who had no interest in the little people. She'd certainly been aloof in high school, spending all her time studying and obsessing what college she would get in to. He'd assumed her life had not changed. Yet, here in her home that wasn't what he saw at all. She was kind, caring and a tad shy.

She didn't even dress like he expected. Worn snug denim hugged her legs and hips giving him the impression of curves he knew he would dream about tonight. Her bulky sweater didn't exactly hide her full breasts either. But it was the look in her eyes when he caught her attention that gave him pause. She alternated between hunger and indifference in the blink of an eye. The woman was clearly in denial. Or simply afraid.

"Here you go." She interrupted his thoughts by handing him a giant margarita glass filled to the brim.

"I hope you don't mind that I didn't salt the rim. I hate the added salt on my drink. But if you want me to add it to yours I can."

"No, this is fine." He took a small sip to appease his hostess. She on the other hand, guzzled half of it in seconds flat. When she came up for air, her eyes opened wide and she snorted.

"Oh my God." She covered her mouth and nose and turned away in apparent horror. "I'm so sorry. I didn't mean to be so rude."

Tucker put down his drink and pulled Maggie onto the couch next to him. "I'm not about to run screaming because Miss Maggie had a rather unladylike moment," he teased.

She closed her eyes and shook her head. "You're never going to quit calling me that are you?"

"Nope. It's an enduring nickname. Why stop now?"

"Oh I don't know. Because we aren't kids anymore?" The wistful tone of her voice struck another chord. Not to mention his instincts demanded he take over and push her to reveal everything she desired. Fortunately for her, he had an iota of preservation and no intention of fucking this up. Maggie deserved a proper introduction, or reintroduction if that was the case, into the seductive nature of a power exchange.

"No, we definitely aren't kids." He brushed a lock of hair from her eyes and tucked it behind her ear. "We're all grown up with real world responsibilities and big boy and big girl desires."

Her mouth opened and closed. "What does that mean?" Her spine straightened and her eyes narrowed, suspicion clouding them.

Good. He liked fire. *A lot.*

"You asked earlier about us catching up. While I don't know every detail, I already know the gist of what you've been up to."

Her jaw went slack moments before he swore steam came out of her ears. "What did you say?"

"It's a small town, Maggie. Even out here on the lake. I doubt your engine cooled in the driveway the day you arrived before the gossip began. Within days of your arrival I'd heard your story mapped out in three different ways. Not to mention the internet."

Her facial expressions changed between horror and outrage. "I don't want to talk about this. I don't care what you've heard. This was such a dumb idea."

"Why? Afraid I plan to condemn you for your choices? You don't know me that well and I am definitely not the boy from high school anymore."

She crunched her face in a frown. "Oh yeah, that's right. You've put me on your bucket list. That's what this is all about isn't it? A notch on your bedpost. A desire to delve outside the norm for a little taste of the dark side from the girl who fucked up so you can put a check mark in your box?"

Tucker tamped the anger surging through his veins. He grabbed the drink from Maggie's hand and placed it on the coffee table without a word. Before she responded, he pushed her back into the couch cushions and came over her. Thigh to thigh, chest to chest. His fingers threaded through her hair and he tugged to get her full attention. "I'm not going to lie and pretend I haven't wanted you from the moment I heard you were back. Hell, you starred in all my teenage fantasies. And yes, you are on my bucket list because that's how long I've waited for you. I may not be what you expected but I may surprise you." To his shock her body softened despite the harsh expression she still wore on her face.

With her silence, he continued. "I am very familiar with your work and what you want and I'm going to take you there and beyond. All you have to do is let go of the fear and say yes."

She winced. "But you don't—"

"What? Understand?" He tightened his grip on her hair and bent to nuzzle the fragrant skin of her neck. He could definitely get lost in little Miss

Maggie. "If you need me to take you to dinner first and spend more time on small talk, just say the word. I can let go of your hair, stop pressing my hard dick into your thigh, and go home. I enjoy a good meal and nice conversation as much as the next guy. Either way will get us to the same destination. You're a submissive wishing for a Dominant and I'm a Dominant looking for one submissive."

CHAPTER THREE

    Maggie swallowed, trying to get his words to sink in. No way in hell had she heard him correctly. Despite her shock, a wave of lust surged through her. Her head spun and her stomach quivered. This was Tucker. The nice boy who had branded her all those years ago with a searing kiss that shocked her to her core. Now he sat on her couch offering her the one thing she secretly ached for. A frown formed across her face. Apparently her desires weren't so secret anymore. The scandal of her life had obviously followed her home.

    She brought her hands to Tucker's chest and pushed. He gave an inch and nothing more. "Don't do this," she whispered. It wasn't easy to form words with the high level of need crashing down on her. What she'd fought for weeks to bottle back up inside her now threatened to break free all over again. She'd been so close to true discovery and then everything crashed and burned around her. An unbelievable case of bad timing had opened her eyes to her ridiculous behavior. Tears burned behind her eyes and she squeezed them shut to hold them at bay. Nothing would embarrass her more than to start crying in front of him.

"Don't do *that*." Tucker's voice whispered through her. "Don't start reinforcing walls and making plans to shut me down. You have nothing to be ashamed of."

Maggie tried to swallow beyond the thick lump in her throat. He didn't know it all. No one did. There had been a lot of speculation about that night. Her ex didn't even care why she'd been in the club, only that she'd been caught there and hauled to jail. He'd used her embarrassment to his advantage, had refused to bail her out and filed for divorce. He'd all but dared her to not sign the settlement agreement, too. Suddenly, all the male students he'd slept with meant nothing in the face of her public scandal.

After days of trying to figure out what to do, she'd grabbed the first opportunity to get out.

Yet none of those memories abated the throbbing now going on between her legs. In an instant, Tucker had managed to reawaken her — gotta have it or I'm going to die — craving that had plagued her for years. The mysterious something else that kept her researching late into the night, page after page on the internet as she tried to understand why she'd become so deeply drawn to the lifestyle.

His proximity didn't help either. Warm breath fluttered across her skin as he waited far too patiently, making her heart beat faster. Good thing she was already sitting down.

"You tell me that I don't know you very well, yet that doesn't stop you from jumping to conclusions about me. For all you know you could be one hundred percent wrong." She hated the sharp edge her voice carried. Her defenses were an auto pilot mechanism she didn't know how to disengage. Not after what she'd been through.

Tucker pulled back and met her gaze. For a few agonizing seconds, silence enveloped them as he stared down at her. She felt as though Tucker could see straight through all of her lies, her half-truths and the walls she'd concocted to hide the need. She admired this Tucker. The confidence that oozed from him was so different from most men she encountered. Most of the professors at the college she worked were ridiculously old school, and not in a good way. They frowned on her research and spent more time offering snide comments than any real support. Not one showed an iota of interest in anything she had to say.

"Look me in the eye, Maggie, and tell me I'm wrong. If you can do that then I'll gladly apologize and drop the whole thing."

Sheer terror sliced through her. Despite her blustering, she liked everything she'd witnessed so far. There were a lot of things in life that made her uncertain, that didn't mean she didn't go for them. That's how the big events in life happened. Sometimes you just have to go for it.

She took a deep breath and slowly exhaled. *Just*

go for it, Maggie. There isn't much else to lose. "You're not wrong," she admitted. For some reason the attack she expected didn't come. Where she'd thought he'd touch her more, he withdrew. Maggie frowned, unable to disguise her confusion.

Tucker cupped her chin with his palm and titled her head to stare into her eyes. "Don't look so disappointed, Miss Maggie. You know as well as I do that this needs to go slow. That means tonight you are going to take a long, hot bath after you finish your drink. You'll wash your body while thinking of me, then you'll slip between the cool sheets of your bed before midnight and go to sleep without touching yourself. You're going to need your sleep."

Her intake of sharp breath caught her off guard. Her body immediately warmed to his instructions and her erogenous zones began to tingle and pulse.

"I mean it, Maggie. No touching. You'll fall asleep with your nipples poking at the thin fabric and moisture pooled between your legs because what you can't yet have is all you'll be able to think about. You'll ache with need and your fingers will clench in frustration as your body riots out of your control. Under no circumstances will you be allowed to touch your pussy or your breasts. Do you understand me?"

Of course she understood, he wanted to torture her. "Why are you doing this?"

"Because it's what I want. Your focus on my

words and desires will please me. When I crawl into my own bed tonight with a dick hard enough to hammer nails, I will feel your pain and know that tomorrow you will come to me for what you need."

"Tomorrow?" she squeaked. It was hard to concentrate on the words she wanted to say when her pulse pounded so hard she thought her chest might burst. She breathed deeply, hoping the extra oxygen would cool the sizzling in her veins. No such luck. Her body buzzed with an electric current that had nowhere to go.

"Yes, Maggie. Tomorrow." His dark eyes held hers in a lock stronger than an invisible force field while his finger traced a path along her check, her neck and across the swell of her breasts.

"Tucker if it's just sex. I don't—" He pressed his fingers to her lips and cut her off before she could continue.

"If it's only about sex, don't follow my directions and don't come to my place tomorrow."

Maggie's pulse jumped. Her legs turned to jelly. The intensity of his words and the way he looked at her in turn both frightened and exhilarated her. He'd turned this into a challenge of trust in a matter of seconds. Either she was willing to accept his offer on his terms or she wasn't. Simple as that. It was her choice.

"So you don't want to have sex then?" She had no idea where the impulse to tease him came from but she couldn't help herself. He'd planted the visuals in her mind with his vivid instructions and she couldn't get them out of her head. She leaned forward until their bodies met. The heat coming from him made her head spin. It wasn't hard to imagine them both standing there without clothes, him ordering her to her knees to suck his cock. A moan slid from her parted lips at the mere thought.

Tucker thrust both hands into her hair and tugged until her head tilted and bared her neck. "You don't want to play games with me, Little One. I'm not above fucking you right here on the floor when pushed."

Maggie gasped. Not in horror, but from the sizzling jolt of lust that coursed through her. Yes, she definitely liked this Tucker.

Before she could respond or make a move, Tucker took control and kissed her senseless. It felt like being thrown into a tornado without warning. His tongue thrust into her mouth and tangled with hers in a firestorm of sensations. Her scalp tingled from the way he held her hair, her breasts ached for his rough touch, and the throb between her legs made her want for so much more.

He didn't let up. He ate at her mouth with such fervor, her body began to shake from the onslaught. Yes, she wanted this so much. Wanted Tucker more than she thought possible. There simply was no question she'd give anything for his domination. She shifted her stance and worked her hand between them in hopes of discovering he wanted her as much as she wanted him. The moment her fingers connected with his cock, he shuddered and broke free.

"As much as I want you under me tonight, I've already laid out my terms. Do you accept?"

Maggie slumped against the wall. "What's wrong with tonight? We're here, we're obviously willing. Why wait?" She suddenly felt more vulnerable than before. Unbalanced. She remembered the anticipation the night at the club and how thrilling that had been but this…him…he was so much more potent.

"Don't get me wrong. I'd love to see you naked for me right now. No doubt about it."

Her heart leapt and her mind soared. Yes!

"However, I'll love it even more tomorrow after you've had a night to anticipate what I'm going to do to you. Besides, my place is much better equipped." He took a step back and she did what she could to hide her disappointment. He wasn't rejecting her…

Wait. What? "Better equipped?"

Tucker nuzzled her throat and scraped his teeth across her neck one last time before he released her and stepped away. "You'll see." He winked.

"I don't even know where you live," she blurted.

"Not a problem." He scooped her small notebook and pen from the coffee table and opened it to a blank page. He quickly scribbled an address and handed it to her. "You know where that is don't you?"

She looked down at the paper and swallowed. She did. Same place he grew up. "You live in your parent's house?"

"Not exactly. Same property, new house. The original house burned and I inherited the property so I rebuilt the guest cabin to suit me."

Fascinating. More curious than ever she couldn't wait to get there. She lifted her head in time to catch him edging toward the door. "You're just going to leave? What about the storm?"

He winked. "Leaving now is for the best and we both know it. Besides the storm isn't really that bad. You unfortunately got caught up in that one spot in the beginning of every rain or snow storm when the roads are most dangerous. Now that there is a little more snow it's actually much easier to drive. You'll see. Tomorrow morning the sunshine will return and the roads will be fine. Especially by noon."

Maggie frowned. There was a part of her that wasn't ready to be separated from him yet. The trembling inside her stomach left her weak, unsure. A touch of anger began to fray along her edges. "This isn't fair. You barge into my life, turn me upside down and inside out and now I'm just supposed to say goodnight, I'll see you tomorrow?"

In the space of a heartbeat his eyes narrowed and he stepped easily into her personal space. "It sounds like you need to think about what you want."

Maggie's stomach dropped and she looked at the floor as if she would see it rolling across the floor in some puddle of humiliation. She was acting like an idiot.

"Look at me." He touched under her chin with his finger and raised her face. The slight twitch at the corners of his mouth the only sign he was not angry. "This is why I'm going home tonight. I hate the thought of you waking up in the morning with regrets. Know this, Maggie, when you come to me tomorrow, and I believe you will, then you will come to me as a submissive to a Dominant."

It wasn't easy to focus on his words. That single touch and the tone of his voice slid through her like molten lava on a steep slope. She couldn't catch her breath in the face of that much power.

"Say, Yes Sir," Tucker prompted.

Her heart skipped a beat. "Yes, Sir," she whispered, afraid she would not be able to speak. Her reaction baffled her. It's not as if she hadn't used the words of respect many times in her research when she interviewed Dominants willing to share their personal details with her. But this felt completely, irrevocably different. Very personal.

"If you need anything, I left my business card next to your phone while you made drinks. I look forward to tomorrow more than you know." With those parting words, Tucker scooped up his keys and disappeared through her front door, leaving her rooted to the spot.

She still couldn't believe what she'd seen and heard with her own eyes and ears. Tucker. Tucker Lewis wanted to dominate her. She crumpled to the floor and landed on her butt with a thud. She sucked in gulp after gulp of air and shook her head, hoping to come to her senses. Her plan to hide out and lick her wounds hadn't lasted very long. She needed water.

Maggie pushed to her feet, scooped up the two margarita glasses and padded into the kitchen. She dumped the contents of the glasses down the drain and placed the empties in the sink. She'd deal with clean up later. First water, and then maybe that long hot soak in the bathtub to clear her head so the could go through the events of the night logically.

She had a lot to think about. *No you don't, dummy.* Maggie stopped in her tracks at her sudden thought. Why did she have to analyze his offer? Tucker wasn't a stranger, she'd been fighting cravings for years, and she no longer had a husband to hold her back. Why shouldn't she simply go for it? She'd spent the better part of her life analyzing every move or decision she made. Maybe it was time to do instead of think. Quit being a scaredy cat who hides behind her work.

Although the last time she'd thrown caution to the wind she'd ended up in jail, without a husband and on sabbatical from a job she… What? Loved? Not much left to love when you strip away the obsession she'd attached to her research. Teaching bored her. It had never sat well with her that she hadn't given her students 110%.

She found her thoughts wandering back to Tucker and wondering what he'd done with his life. Besides rescuing women by the side of the road, what did he do? She vaguely remembered something about a scholarship. She racked her brain trying to remember the details but couldn't remember what school he'd accepted or what he'd planned to study. Senior year had been a whirlwind and she and Derek had experienced a tumultuous relationship. Later, when she'd started her research, she'd concluded that Derek had recognized her submissive tendencies and while trying to act on them he'd failed miserably. Even as a teenager he'd been a good guy and he'd stuck with her through senior prom before breaking up with her. To her current shame, she'd been so wrapped up in her own world, she couldn't remember much at all about Tucker in those last months.

Tomorrow, she'd rectify that situation. He'd made her body come to life at the speed of sound, but that didn't mean her mind wasn't engaged. She wanted to know more about the man who'd set the bar for every kiss she ever received.

For now, she had some instructions to follow. She straightened her spine and strode toward the bathroom. The self pity and river of denial ended tonight.

CHAPTER FOUR

Tucker fiddled with the brushes and paints on his table, unable to get the exact color mix he sought. He wanted something the color of Maggie's eyes when arousal had slammed into her. Specifically, the darker hue that surrounded the edges of her pupils. He longed to paint her, despite portraits not being his usual style. She presented a conundrum in so many ways. An interesting mix of inquisitive, no-nonsense professor on the outside and soft submissive on the inside. While he enjoyed the two facets, it was the inside he wanted to discover today. He couldn't wait to get to the heart of what she'd desired all these years.

Did she know that Derek used to complain about her in high school? To everyone else she'd seemed aloof; to her then-boyfriend she was a pushover. Derek had let all his friends know that she liked being told what to do. Most teenagers didn't know what that meant but Tucker had a pretty good idea. The other guys had laughed it off as if she was some sort of doormat. That inside knowledge from Derek may have been what drove

Tucker to kiss her that night. He wanted her so bad, he'd ached. Her eager response had thrown him for a loop.

Tucker shook his head and banished the past from his thoughts. That was a long time ago and neither of them resembled the kids of their youth. She'd gone into a structured profession that came with a lot of history and rigid rules. He imagined what she'd looked like in a buttoned down conservative business suit. Or more importantly, what she'd look like with her suit jacket and blouse unbuttoned to the waist, her breasts bound so as to keep them aroused and available to his mouth and hands. Fuck. His fantasies were going to kill him. He'd never spent a day of his life working in a normal office but for a chance at getting Maggie bound and bent over a desk he might rethink his career goals.

Poor Maggie. Her rules had worked for her for a while until she'd pushed at her boundaries a little too hard and it all blew up in her face. He'd be willing to bet none of her fellow professors had cornered her in her office and drilled her for the truth about her sexuality. Why else would she be in trouble now? There was no doubt her history fascinated him. He couldn't stop thinking about everything she'd been through, and more importantly, where she wanted to go now. Where he wanted to take her.

He turned to the blank canvas and pondered

what had driven him to this room. Generally, he spent more time outside in his workshop. He reveled in the heat and power that infused him when he worked with fired glass. What had started out as a strange hobby to distract him from the dark pit he'd fallen into had turned into a secret profession that now afforded him a level of peace his abandoned attempt at club owner never could. Tucker scowled. He hated that the memory of the life he'd walked away from still plagued him. Ten long years had passed since he'd returned home to the nightmare of his father's legacy and after an extended stint in a hell of his own making, he'd clawed his way back to the land of the living where he hoped to recapture the missing piece of his life.

Yeah, this trip down memory lane was not making his day. He didn't want Maggie's visit to be influenced by the things he'd done in the past. She wasn't an anonymous submissive whose only job was to temporarily smother the resentment burning inside him. Those days were safely behind him. From the moment he'd seen her illuminated in the snow, his thoughts were consumed with various ways to give her pleasure. He turned to the Saint Andrews cross in the far corner of the room and imagined Maggie naked and restrained. He longed to work her to the brink of sexual insanity before he began to capture her image with brush and paint.

It had been a long time since he'd invited anyone into his studio playroom, and the first time he longed to paint someone. The toys in here had gathered dust to the point he'd spent all morning restoring his tools of the trade to their former glory and rearranging the chest he used to keep everything neat. To his dismay he had to throw away more than a dozen floggers that were beyond repair. If things worked out with Maggie, he'd commission some new ones, made specifically for her. His thoughts were immediately drawn back to what her skin looked like. Pale and translucent simply waiting for someone to—

Tucker's phone buzzed on his hip, signaling someone had arrived at his front door. He dismissed the security app from his cell screen and headed out of his private studio and into the main house. Almost the entire building featured windows, so he easily saw from the back of the house to the front door. His cock stirred in anticipation. Leaving Maggie last night had been one of the hardest things he'd ever done and she'd consumed his thoughts since he left her. Giving them both the night to anticipate was the right thing to do. However, the wait was now over and they could get on with the incredible scene he expected.

At the front entrance he counted to ten. Once he was fully in control, he opened the door.

"I'm so glad you came." He held out his hand and waited.

"I wasn't sure I would until I literally got in the car and started driving." She placed her small hand in his and let him draw her through the door.

"Nervous?" She didn't have to answer for him to know. The slight tremble of her hand clued him in.

"A little," she admitted.

Tucker wrapped his arm around her waist and pulled her tight against his frame. For a moment he reveled in the softness of her body. He breathed in the barely there scent of her perfumed skin and savored the gift she'd already given him. Most people forgot to savor every moment. Once upon a time he too had been guilty of that. No longer. Her arrival at his door offered him a taste of the trust he'd been eager to receive.

God, it's been so long.

"Come inside and I'll see what I can do about that." He led her toward the small living room where he took a seat on the sofa and pulled her into his lap.

She squeaked in surprise.

"Relax, I only want to talk for a few minutes." He brushed his thumb across the tender skin between her thumb and forefinger in a steady pattern. He needed to soothe and reassure as much as she needed to receive it. The significance of small touches was never lost on him. In fact, it was the little things that always made a scene stand out in his mind.

"There is nothing to fear. We won't do anything that really frightens you," he assured all while he continued to stroke her.

When her rigid muscles started to relax under his ministrations, he began. "Have you tried BDSM before? Maybe in your marriage?" He didn't relish bringing up the subject of her past but he needed to know how much practical experience she had versus book knowledge. They were worlds apart in his eyes and with Maggie, he was determined to avoid any potential minefields. Or at least plow through them now, so he didn't end up surprised by a sudden detonation mid scene later.

She shook her head. "Not at all. I—uh—" She bit her bottom lip.

Tucker leaned back on the couch and watched her reactions. She interlocked her fingers and held them in her lap, her eyes darted around the room looking anywhere but at him, and her foot began a barely noticeable tapping on the hardwood floors. There was definitely something she wasn't telling him and from the looks of it she wasn't eager to spill her secrets.

"The more I know before we get started the better the experience. Nothing would hurt me more than to do something that hurt you. I'd much rather spend my day giving you pleasure." Even if the route to pleasure happened to be through some aspects of pain. He longed to experiment with different levels until he found her threshold.

"I—I— don't think I would like spanking," she blurted.

Interesting. "Because…" he prompted. Maybe if

he dug deeper he could move her beyond her hesitation.

"Because it is not erotic to be treated like a child who has done something bad. And I don't think reenacting that is romantic or sexy."

Tucker nodded but filed that information away for further discussion. There was no need to rush and he certainly wasn't going to belittle her feelings. "What about flogging? I've been told by many subs they find it almost therapeutic during a scene." He rubbed his hand down her thighs and back up again. Her lush figure entranced him.

"No hitting." She twisted in his arms to face him. "Believe me, I know how weird that sounds to someone into BDSM. And I understand if that's a deal breaker for you. I'm very aware it's one of the most popular activities practiced in the lifestyle and can only imagine how disappointing my limit must be."

Her voice rose an octave and her spine straightened. He might not yet understand her objections but he certainly found her getting her back up about it quite arousing. Mentally he scratched off the rack of floggers and whips as appropriate implements for the day. He'd have to get more creative until he was ready to push her further.

"Anything else you don't like?"

She shrugged. "I don't think I'll know until I try

something." To her horror, her voice cracked on the last part. She'd expected him to be canceling their plans by now. It had been easy to knock on the door knowing full well he'd reject her issues.

"I would bet that in your research, you've either read about or seen more than the average newbie. What turned you on?" He reached for the edge of her long skirt and hiked it up to her thighs.

Maggie tried to keep her thoughts on his question but he made it really difficult to concentrate when his fingers connected to the bare skin of her inner thighs. What would he think of her when he discovered she'd skipped underwear? "I'm fascinated by a woman tied up." She felt the heat of a blush creep up the front of her neck. There was no reason a seasoned professor such as herself should be blushing like a ridiculous schoolgirl.

"I'm pleased to hear that." His fingers inched higher and squeezed. Maggie held her breath and prayed he couldn't hear the mad thrumming of her pulse. To her it sounded like an ocean through a megaphone. Loud and wild. "What else?" He feathered his fingers across the lips of her pussy. The barely there touch ignited a firestorm inside her, causing her to clench her teeth and breathe deep.

"Not — not sure." Forget talking, she needed him to touch her before she started to cry — or worse — beg. The pulse of her clit bordered on painful, her nipples tightened beyond expectation and moisture coated the edges of her sex. One touch. Yes, please.

One touch.

"You can do this." He slid a finger between her folds and teased her opening. "Did I mention how much I love that you didn't wear underwear today?" A little more teasing and his finger dipped inside. "In fact, as sexy as some panties are, I'd prefer if you never wore them."

Maggie's heart skipped a beat. Her muscles tensed. This was Tucker who held her in his lap, sliding his finger in and out of her pussy. How the hell was she supposed to stay detached in this? How could she not? A bitter divorce still hung heavy on her mind, not to mention the current shambles of her career.

"Stop it!" His voice boomed through the room. "Whatever you're thinking about that made you tense up has got to go."

"But I—"

Tucker slipped his free hand across her mouth and stopped her protest cold. "Don't bother. I think we've had enough talking for now. Here are the rules. First, no talking is permitted unless I ask you a direct question. Understood?"

"Yes," she answered.

"Actually Yes, Sir would be the appropriate response. But you already knew that didn't you?" He uncovered her mouth and waited.

She hesitated for half a second before she amended her response. "Yes, Sir." It surprised her how easy the word *Sir* rolled from her tongue. She'd waited what felt like half her life for someone who wanted to hear it, and kind of expecting she'd hate saying it.

"That's better." He trailed his fingers along her cheek, across her jaw line and slowly wrapped his hand around her neck. He did not squeeze or tighten, yet the power in his grip was unmistakable.

"Second, you'll pick a safe word that you won't hesitate to use if you can't take anymore. I don't know what you've seen before, but using a safe word is not a sign of weakness or a signal that we can no longer continue at a later time. It's a safety tool, plain and simple. So don't assume anything more or less if you need to use it."

He hadn't stopped moving his finger inside her and it took every ounce of willpower to focus on his words more than the sensations he created.

"I don't want to hurt you, Maggie. Except in ways that will lead to pleasure for us both. Do you want me to continue?"

His finger brushed a particular responsive spot and she gasped. Continue? Was he kidding? She felt pinned in place, desperate for more and it was far more pleasant than she expected. If he stopped now she might kill him.

"Yes." A breath after she spoke the word she remembered. "Sir."

"Very nice. Your honest and easy response tells me a lot."

Maggie closed her eyes and tried not to think

about how natural this became by the minute. She was so damned horny now. Anything he wanted she was prepared to give so long as he kept going. A breath later, his hand stilled between her legs.

"Oh no. Please don't stop."

A low chuckle rumbled against her back. "I think that's exactly what I need to do." He removed his hand and lifted her to a standing position in front of him.

Maggie frowned. "That's not very nice," she complained.

"Nice isn't the goal now is it? Don't answer that. All I require right now is your nudity. Take off your clothes, Maggie and then lower your body to your knees. I wish to see every inch of you."

Maggie's stomach quivered at the tone of his request. Standing with her back to Tucker left her unsure what to do next. Part of her wanted to bolt before she lost complete control and the other part stood rooted to the floor unable to move. He'd made her an offer and she'd accepted, so why did the sudden image of being way in over her head keep popping up?

"I'm waiting, sub." The gruff sound of his voice might have put her off and ended their scene before it started if she hadn't heard the slight hitch in his breath. The sudden knowledge that Tucker Lewis sat staring at her back just as affected as she, filled her with enough confidence to keep going.

She reached for the button of her skirt, lowered

the zipper, and slid the soft fabric over her hips and legs until it pooled on the floor at her feet. With his gaze likely boring into her backside, she lifted her blouse over her head and tossed it to the end of the couch. She waited for him to say something, even strained to hear his breathing, before she continued. Instead the silence thickened and somehow made it easier for her to go on.

When her bra fell to the ground and her breasts sprang free, she moaned. Cool air rushed over her elongated and erect nipples making them ache more than before. Tension coiled in her stomach and between her thighs. He hadn't said a word and she was already shaking. The muscles of her thighs quivered as she contemplated what to do next. He'd said on her knees but not seeing his reaction was killing her.

"May I turn?" She held her breath.

"No."

The one word response startled her. This was it. The next move was completely up to her. She could either comply with his demands or end it now. Who was she kidding? She'd come this far…

Maggie bent to the floor and as gracefully as possible got down on her knees. She tried to keep perfectly still as she waited for Tucker to instruct her further. What she wanted to do was turn, check to see if he was actually still interested. Maybe he'd changed his mind when she'd removed her clothing. She hadn't exactly kept up with her exercise schedule.

"Is this hard for you, little one? Sitting still and waiting for your Dom to tell you what's next?"

Her Dom? Her stomach quivered at the thought. This was really happening. "I'm fine," she answered. What a lie.

A firm hand nudged at her back until she gave in to the pressure and allowed him to press her head to the floor.

"Are you now?" His hand reached under her bottom, one finger sliding through the increased moisture of her sex. "You're certainly wet."

Maggie had no response. What the hell could she say? He had the evidence of her desire on his fingers. With one hand on her back holding her to the ground and the other exploring her pussy, she'd pretty much give anything if he'd fuck her now. The need for him to take her quick and hard for his pleasure speared through her like lightening. Unfortunately his hand wandered down her thigh and behind her knee.

"Don't pretend to be tougher than you are. With me you are free to be the woman inside. There is no judgment in these walls. Today you'll learn there is nothing, no response, no emotion that you can hide from me. I'll take and you'll give with no restraint. The pleasure will be ours. Together."

The pit of Maggie's stomach quivered. For the tenth time since she'd left her house she was certain she'd jumped off the face of a cliff with no safety cord. By now fear should have paralyzed her and instead she practically melted into the floor. In the back of her mind she heard the distinct sound of leather sliding against leather and imagined Tucker removing his belt. She tried to sit and found his grip tighter than she expected. She'd not moved an inch. She turned her head to the side and hoped upon hope to catch something from the corner of her eye.

Frustrated, she blew out a hard breath. He might as well have blindfolded her. The sound of his zipper came next, torturing her senses. In her mind's eye she saw Tucker reach into his pants and draw out his thick, hard penis until it jutted boldly from his hips. Would he remove the slacks or fuck her as is with his pants on and her body folded on the ground.

She cried out when her pussy muscles clenched violently. With her breath sawing in and out of her lungs as she tried to control her reactions, a thick finger breached the tight opening of her sex. This time he wasn't light and easy. He thrusted roughly inside her, creating sharp friction that nearly sent her careening over the edge. Oh God. So close.

"Yes. Yes. Yes," she whimpered, her hips gyrating against his hand. "Tucker, I—ohh—I…"

Seconds later she found her body pinned in place by his legs as he towered over her. Then his chest was against her back and his free hand wrapped underneath her. Instead of touching her clit like she'd hoped, he brushed against her stomach in a trail to her breast. There he grasped a nipple and pinched. Delicious torment that grew tighter and tighter until… "Owwww!" she screamed. Blinding pain swept through her nipple and breast in a direct line to her pussy. There the heat gave way to pleasure and her body drew taught. So much pleasure, so much more still not there. Only a little more and she'd fly free.

His fingers eased on her nipple and she didn't know whether to sigh a breath of relief or cry for the injustice of it all. She didn't have long to consider before he moved to the other nipple and repeated the same move. Another scream tore through her throat and she bucked wildly against his hand.

"What is happening?" she cried.

"I'm watching you come apart in my arms, little one. And what a beautiful sight it is." His grip tightened and the pulse at her clit throbbed incessantly.

"Oh. My. God. I'm so close." She couldn't think about anything but the intensity of the pleasure he created. Fuck.

"I know. Which is why I have to stop." He released her breast and withdrew the finger he'd used to fuck her pussy.

"What? Wait." With all her strength, Maggie muscled her way free and flopped to her side. "Why the hell would you—?" The question died on her lips at the sight of Tucker's weeping cock. Thick viscous fluid coated the dark mushroom head making her mouth water. She licked her lips and moved closer.

Strong arms wrapped around her waist and lifted her from the ground before she'd moved a foot from her position. "If you truly don't want to feel my belt on your backside, you'll stop struggling."

She immediately froze despite the extra quiver she felt deep in her pussy. Her nipples ached, distracting her further. What the hell was wrong with her? She wasn't supposed to react like this when he threatened her with the one thing she disliked.

To make things worse he stroked one of her breasts with a light caress that brought her as much pleasure as the pinch had. She sighed and relaxed again.

"Fighting it won't help. It might delay the inevitable but eventually I'll have my way and you'll get where you need to go. I promise you that."

Maggie clenched her jaw and remained silent. It felt childish but she wasn't happy to be denied.

"There are things I can do that will bring you more pleasure than you can imagine. All you have to do is let me take care of you. Trust that whatever I do is designed for both our enjoyment. Be open."

"I've never let anyone take care of me."

"I know. That's why your surrender will be all the more sweet to a man like me."

"This messes with my head. I don't know how to react."

He chuckled. "You had to expect that. With all the time you spent on research. I'm sure you've heard it explained a thousand times. What you didn't understand is that no amount of book learning can prepare you for how it really feels."

Maggie didn't particularly enjoy her sudden cowardice. She'd pursued the lifestyle with a passion that easily bordered on obsession. How easily things changed when the tables were turned on her.

Tucker lowered her to her feet while keeping her cradled in his arm. "Since you look at a loss for words, I think it's time to move onto the second item on our agenda."

"You have an agenda?"

He shifted his arms and released her. To her disappointment he pushed his cock back into his pants and zipped them back up. "I am nothing if not meticulous in my attention to details."

Maggie bit her tongue to keep her smart response to herself. She definitely got the impression she was on the verge of pushing her luck.

"This way." He grabbed her hand and began leading her to the back of the house.

"What about my clothes? Don't I need to put them on?"

"No." He glanced down at her scattered items. "They are staying right where they are for the foreseeable future."

"That's not fair. You're fully dressed."

Without a word Tucker turned a 100-watt smile on her that left her quaking in front of him. The man was gorgeous when he did that, but it was nothing compared to the devilish look in his eye. That look said I am the devil and you are my prey and there isn't a damn thing you can do about it.

CHAPTER FIVE

Tucker led her from the house, across a small glass enclosed breezeway and into his very private space. He needed these few minutes to get his body under control and to think through a few changes from his earlier plans. It would be so easy to lose himself in this incredible woman. First things first, he wanted her bound and unable to move much. She needed him to take complete control and what better way to accomplish that than to leave her bound and waiting while he sketched.

"What's all this?"

Her question brought him out of his own head and placed his attention back on her where it should be. "I guess you could call it my combination home office and playroom."

He watched her gaze wander the space from the messy desk and piles of sketchpads to the play equipment he'd let gather dust for quite some time.

"You work in here with that big St. Andrew's cross suspended in the middle of the room?" She'd zoomed in on his favorite piece of equipment.

"Not usually. It's easy to move out of the way when I don't need it. Today I'll need it."

Her steps faltered and that deer in the headlights look crossed her face again. There was a certain appeal to her apprehension. He tugged her arm and spun her into his arms until her front squashed against his chest. "When I enter this room it's a trigger to leave the world behind. Forget stress. Forget people. Forget whatever it is that bothers me. Like me, in here you'll be free to be whatever you want, however you want, whomever you want."

"Don't you mean I'll be free to do whatever you want me to?"

He cupped her chin and lifted her head. "I know you understand the basic concepts of BDSM. That knowledge is good to have, but there is a time and place for your sass. Now is not that time. Do you understand?"

She nodded.

He sighed. "Not good enough, Maggie. Do you understand?"

He watched the muscle at her jaw line jump for a few seconds as she debated giving him what he wanted. Finally she spoke, "Yes, Sir. I understand."

"Much better." He stroked a finger along one bare arm to the crook of her elbow. From there he moved to a plump breast and squeezed. Yes, she felt very good indeed. Gorgeous long nipples simply begging for his attention, tits that fit perfectly in his hands and an underlying eagerness to please that spoke volumes without a word.

He dipped his head and sucked a nipple into his mouth. Her gasp, other than being music to his ears, prompted him to keep going. He laved the puckered skin with repeated licks that made small whimpers sound in her throat. He liked the idea that she'd be very noisy when she came. Nothing got him going like a submissive's scream. And as far as he was concerned the louder the better.

He moved on from her right breast with a pop and repeated his treatment on the left while his hand worked the other. Her hands threaded through his hair and tugged him closer. Tucker growled and bit the tip of her nipple while allowing her an ample amount of free reign for now. This was her first foray into a BDSM scene and he'd have her bound and helpless soon enough. Then she'd learn.

After a few minutes, the hunger clawing his insides grew insistent. With his nose buried between her breasts and the scent of her skin changing as they went, the need for so much more began driving him slowly mad. "I need to be inside you," he whispered against her flesh.

"Tucker," she moaned.

He liked the sound of his name on her lips. He liked Sir and eventually Master even better. Ready for more, he skimmed his hand along her hip and thigh to the small patch of trimmed hair between her legs. Her breath caught and he smiled. She was going to be so much fun.

Tucker withdrew his hand and took a step back. Maggie cried out in protest and her body sagged. He grabbed her around the waist and steadied her on her feet.

"Is this what I should expect from you, Tucker Lewis? Cruelty? Constant taunting?"

"Aww, C'mon Miss Maggie. Teasing is fun." He walked her toward the large metal wheel in the center of the room. "Stand right here," he ordered.

She turned and looked behind her for a second before returning to meet his gaze. "Am I getting on that thing?"

"Do you want to? I think you'll like it."

She fidgeted, shifting her body weight from one foot to the other. Tucker crouched down and dug into the leather bag he'd left earlier at the base of the structure. He grabbed the soft leather cuffs he'd arranged on top and began buckling them around Maggie's wrists.

"Don't worry, little one. I'm going to be right here with you the whole time and if you'd like I can talk you through everything one step at a time."

The pulse at the base of her throat jumped and his cock hardened a fraction more, though he didn't know how. He already ached to bursting and would give anything to drop his plans and simply fuck her first to take the edge off.

He finished attaching the cuffs and wrapped his hands around her face and brought her close. "What's going through that beautiful head of yours, darling? You're going to have to share."

"I'm nervous, that's all."

Tucker narrowed his gaze. "Is that really all? If you're not comfortable talking to me we can stop and try again some other time."

"No," she cried. "I mean — please. I'll be fine."

"I know you will, baby. You've thought about this for a long time haven't you?" He traced a finger around the edges of her lips, focusing on the beauty of the pale pink lushness of her mouth.

"Not exactly."

Tucker chuckled. "No, I would guess not. I meant the being tied up part, the submitting to a Dominant," he ventured. "The choice of partner is a bit newer."

She nodded.

"Tell me what you think submission is?" he asked. They'd start there and then move on.

"The act of yielding to the will of another," she replied in a monotone voice.

"Spoken like a true professor." He pulled an arm behind her back. "Grab that bar."

She hesitated, her mouth opening and closing. Tucker curved his hand around the side of her neck and steered her focus back to him. "Say it."

Maggie scrunched up her nose and bit her lip.

Tucker leaned forward and pressed against her soft frame. "I mean it, Maggie. I want to hear every word going through your head right now. If during our play, I decide you need to hold your tongue, I'll definitely let you know. So say it."

He leaned back and watched her shoulders straighten.

"I may not have any practical experience but I'm not stupid. It doesn't take play to understand what something means or to feel it inside."

Tucker let her words digest for a moment before he responded. Her intelligence was both a blessing and a barrier. At least for now. "Relax, Maggie. I don't disagree with you at all and I'm not going to try to correct how you feel." He brushed his nose along her cheek and nuzzled behind her ear. "Quite the contrary. I only want to prove it's even more than you've imagined. At the end of the day I want you curled on your side with my arm wrapped around you, your body tucked to mine and your mind only able to register how content you are. My motives are that simple."

Before she could respond, he grabbed her opposite hand and pulled it behind her back. "Grab the bar."

She complied and after he fastened her wrists to the bar with leather straps, he stood back to admire her stance. With both hands forced behind her back to grab the cross bar, her chest pushed forward and her luscious nipples pointed into the air.

Her ability to still follow his directions while questioning his motives left a knowing mark. Unconsciously she wanted to submit as much, if not more than her mind even knew.

"Submission is exactly what you said it was. However, the clinical definition will give way to something a bit more indescribable during play if things go well between us."

"If?" Her voice trembled.

Tucker stroked a lone finger along her cheek and dipped the tip of his finger between her lips. "Yes, Maggie. There is always the possibility that at some point it will become too much for you. That's what a safe word is for. Do you have one?"

"No, not really." Her eyes cast in the opposite direction.

He tucked his finger behind her teeth like a hook and tugged her jaw until she was forced to look at him. "No what?" he asked.

Confusion clouded her eyes for a moment before her mistake dawned on her. "No, Sir," she replied.

"Much better. Keep it simple today. I'm not planning to judge you. So pick a safe word then. Something easy to remember but not often used in your daily life. It can't be a word that would come up in a normal conversation."

"Love," she blurted.

Tucker winced. He knew as well as the next psychologist that a sudden word association like that came with meaning. She'd been hurt and whether she'd fully recovered or not, there were scars. For now he'd tread carefully.

"I was thinking something a bit more unusual, like aardvark."

Maggie stared at him for a few seconds, blinked and then broke out in laughter. The rich lilting sound went a long way to relieving some of the tension he'd begun to feel. While he had complete confidence in his ability to carry out the scene, he felt an urgent need to get this right. Maggie had to be different than all the rest.

All the rest.

Tucker refused to go there. Today was his and Maggie's fresh start.

"Can we just stick with red? If I need you to stop that's more likely what I'm going to say."

While he'd been wandering in his thoughts, Maggie had stopped laughing and grown serious. Her flushed face drew his attention again. "Yes, red works. I'm not a stickler for protocols, I simply want you to feel safe to explore anything and everything you desire."

"Thank you, Sir" Her head dropped when she spoke the words in a soft voice.

He didn't think he could hide his grin of satisfaction this time, so he turned to the small antique cabinet behind him where he stored many of his beloved toys. He opened the middle drawer and scooped up the nipple clamps he'd picked out for her over a week ago. They'd arrived in the mail just in time.

He was ready to get started.

Maggie looked up just in time to see Tucker turn around with something in his hands. Fortunately he didn't leave her waiting as he opened each palm to show two nipple clamps with small purple beads dangling from the clip.

Oh dear. The silliness she'd been experiencing a moment ago fizzled out and her heart began to pick up speed. With her clothes somewhere in the house and her wrists and ankles shackled to this weird wheel, a sudden sense of vulnerability crept over her. Until now she'd managed to keep it light and stay calm. Not anymore.

He stepped close. So close she swore she felt the air shift between them every time he moved. His dark gaze bored into her as his hands began to roam over her naked body with the cool beads that somehow left a trail of heat every where he touched.

For a few seconds, serious doubts began to plague her. Was she sure? Was she crazy? She opened her mouth to say something and no sound came out. Her protests died in her throat because Tucker began teasing her nipples with the tips of his fingers.

She liked it a lot when he pinched them. The tiny burst of pain had knifed through her as fast as a lightning strike and as equally devastating.

"Tucker I—"

His lips brushed the shell of her ear. "Shhh. I'm going to put these on your nipples now. Then I'm going to step back and admire how lovely you look shackled and clamped."

The feel of his rough skin on the slope of her right breast caught her breath. She'd noticed the myriad of scars on both of his hands earlier and found the difference in texture fascinating. Rough against smooth. Raw wood against silk. Her thoughts jumbled, refusing her the ability to put a string of words together in a sentence.

"Keep breathing. There's no reason to hold your breath yet."

That's exactly what she was worried about. The *yet* part.

With two fingers he squeezed and rolled her nipple. That same sizzling sensation erupted around her clit. It seemed so unrealistic that such a small touch on a totally different part of the body would make her pussy quiver. Her head lolled to the side.

"I love that you're so responsive to my touch. As soon as your eyes roll back in your head, I can read you like a book."

She slowly opened her lids at his words. Her stomach tumbled the minute her gaze locked with his. The heat between her legs spread until she started to squirm.

"Now you're ready." He didn't wait for a response or give her another second to breathe. He clipped the small mouth of the clamp over her extended left nipple and let go.

Maggie sucked in a breath at the sharp bite of

pain that erupted at the site.

"Look at me." The stern tone of his voice caught her attention and she eagerly obeyed. Immediately the heat in his gaze shot through her. He liked what he saw. "The worst of the bite is already easing. Just relax and let the pressure do the work."

Maggie followed his directions and forced her muscles to go lax. And he was right. The pain had lessened somewhat and she'd been too busy on her way to a freak out to realize it. He ran his hand around the areola and squeezed gently. "You have perfect nipples for clamps. I'm going to enjoy playing with them."

She groaned. The more he talked the more she sank into the experience. Her arousal already high, spiked further as a sense of urgency stole over her.

"Thank you, Sir." She didn't know what else to say. No words came to her to describe how incredible she felt at the moment and asking him to do as he pleased…

Her train of thought cut off when Tucker wrapped his hand around the back of her neck and threaded his fingers in her hair seconds before he covered her mouth with his. Soft lips flattened against her mouth and he slipped his tongue inside to slide alongside hers.

When she thought she'd collapse from a simple kiss, he plumped her free nipple between two fingers until little mewls sounded from deep inside her. Lost in the pleasure curling through her, Tucker caught her off guard when he fastened the second clamp onto her breast.

Maggie tore free from his kiss. She panted through the pain, waiting for a similar easing as the last one. When it didn't come she looked up at Tucker to find him smiling.

"It hurts."

"Yes, pet. It should. The combination of both nipples clamped at the same time creates a totally different sensation than only one. Just keep breathing and you'll be fine."

For some reason her brain focused on the fact he'd called her pet instead of the pain. Something shifted inside her. She'd never been one for nicknames but when he called her "Miss Maggie" or now "pet" a slow warmth crept through her. She liked it.

"Let your brain think beyond your nipples now." He ambled around her, his fingertips gliding over her bare skin. "Think about your belly." His fingers splayed across her abdomen. "Feel the quiver of the muscles as I touch you there."

Maggie held her breath. Every cell in her body fired to life like little rocket flares exploding in the night sky. Extreme. Exciting.

"I love the curve of your waist and hip right here." His hands grabbed the indentation of her waist and skimmed down to her thighs. "I long to feel my hips cradled between your legs." To her pleasure, he massaged her quads, loosening some of the tension she'd built up over her ordeal.

She sighed and relaxed back on the odd contraption he'd attached her to. "Is this really necessary right now?" Maggie tugged on the restraints at her wrists. "You're turning me to jello."

He simply raised his eyebrows and dropped his hands.

Whatever he had planned for her, that one look reminded her that he was in control now not her. Instead of her normal instinct to argue or withdraw, Maggie closed her eyes and relaxed on a long sigh. Giving into his will.

"Good girl."

Maggie opened her eyes and met his gaze, amazed by the warmth he once again offered. "That's what you were waiting for wasn't it?"

He stared at her for a long moment, his gaze so intent she felt as if he'd crawled inside her and opened a new door.

"Of course. Now I can begin."

Instead of touching her again like she ached for, Tucker turned and strode across the room. Straight to a — an easel? What the hell?

When he lifted his head and looked at her, he frowned. "Don't look so disappointed, Miss Maggie. I've thought about this for so long I have to get it down on paper." He grabbed some charcoal from the small table next to him and began to scratch on the paper.

Maggie stood motionless, still shocked he'd brought her here for his art. This wasn't what she'd expected at all. Some of the warmth she'd been feeling receded and the pain at her nipples throbbed a bit more incessantly. Her pussy ached too. Now that he'd turned his attention to the piece of paper in front of him she realized how wet she'd become as he'd coaxed her into position.

"Tucker, I don't think. I mean I'm not sure about this."

He didn't look up. "Unless you address me properly here in this room, I'm not going to respond."

She ground her teeth in frustration. She'd forgotten again.

"You have a beautiful body, Maggie. It's very inspiring." He paused, captured her gaze for a few breathless seconds, and then with a frown continued to sketch.

Minutes passed and neither of them said anything. He worked furiously and she tried to think of something other than the fact she stood strapped to a wooden contraption with her nipples clamped. More importantly she desperately wanted to ease the ache between her legs. The streaks of constant pain from her nipples still ran a direct line to her clit and every few minutes her sex squeezed with an ache to be filled that startled her.

"Sir," she started and stopped.

He immediately turned his attention to her.

"Yes, my pet?"

"Is this supposed to be some sort of punishment?"

Tucker dropped his chalk, wiped his hands on a cloth and walked over to her. "Why would you think that? We haven't even discussed whether this relationship will include such things."

Her gaze slid over him as he moved. The black V-neck sweater molded to his upper body enough to show off a chest she longed to rub against. In the heat of his work, he'd pushed the sleeves to his elbows and her gaze was drawn to the hair sprinkled across his forearms. The soft smoke gray pants he wore did little to hide his massive erection as he approached. Just staring at him made it impossible to think straight.

"I hurt. I don't know what to do."

"If the clamps are unbearable you only need say so." He reached for one and she jerked away.

"No," she cried. "That's not what I mean."

His grin spread across his face quickly and Maggie frowned. As soon as he'd understood what she meant he seemed to like that idea entirely too much.

He put his hand between her legs and slowly ran a finger through her wet folds. "I do love a hot and wet submissive." Back and forth he rubbed, being careful not to touch her now puffy clit.

Maggie's head spun and the world around her tilted. Part of her wanted to protest and wipe the smug look from his face and the other, more important part of her, thought she'd die if he stopped. She fought the restraints, first her arms and then her legs. It was much harder than she'd thought to stay calm when she'd reached such a fever pitch.

"Be still, Maggie. Don't fight this."

His level tone broke through the beginnings of her panic and she stopped moving. Her legs shook as his fingers explored more of her sex. First circling, the protruding hot spot and then around her entrance. She tried to keep quiet, even going so far as to bite her lip. But he was driving her insane.

When he pushed a finger inside, she cried out. Sweet heaven that felt good.

"Mmm," he murmured. "I can only imagine how incredible you'd feel around my dick."

His earthy words sent Maggie's pulse into overdrive, beating a harsh rhythm in her ears. His finger pushed deeper and she swore she saw flashes of light at the edge of her vision. He'd strung her so tight the slightest touch was setting her off.

He reached for her breast with his other hand and Maggie tried to brace herself for the added sensations to no avail. His hand tugged at the small fall of beads and a low wail erupted from her throat.

Holy shit! She was literally going to go insane with need. Her body pulsed, her sex squeezed and her stomach quivered uncontrollably. The gathering orgasm pulsed forward.

"So close," he said seconds before his touch disappeared. "Right where you need to be for your next lesson.

What? Was he crazy?

Tucker returned to the small cabinet near the wall and pulled a crop from a bottom drawer. The slender black implement with its small piece of leather at the end intimidated her. If she thought she had her doubts before, they were twofold now when faced with the real deal. The really scary thing was in the fact that her distaste of such things from her research was quickly giving way to a desire to feel, to please, and to experience the pleasure Tucker had promised.

"What are you going to do?" Her voice trembled.

"Probably not exactly what you're thinking. Although I do think it's important to push past your preconceived notions and see first hand if you enjoy it." He touched the leather tip to her stomach with a barely there brush. "Life's too short to live in wonder, Maggie."

The sudden sadness in his eyes shocked her. Was he still talking about her?

"I need to touch you," she paused. "Sir."

"I know you do and I promise you will, when the time is right." He trailed the crop down her hip and the side of her leg all the way to her ankle. "Right now I want to touch you like this. Are there any triggers I should know about that make you reluctant to enjoy my crop?"

"Triggers?" She could barely breath. That feather light touch of leather he continued to apply to her naked body made a rush of need sweep through her. Want.

"Yes. Like any bad experiences that made you afraid of a whip or a spanking." He hesitated his strokes.

She shook her head. "No. Just. I just—just can't wrap my head around it."

He laughed. "Bet you're starting to wrap that pretty head around it now." He'd begun tapping the end of the crop against the outside of her thigh in a rhythmic pattern. Before long he tapped across her leg to the inside where more sensitive skin lay.

Maggie wanted something so badly she didn't know whether to cry or beg. Tears of frustration formed in her eyes.

"It's okay, pet. Let the emotion wash over you. Trust that I've got you." He nudged her wet folds with the crop all while continuing that crazy tapping. She held her breath when he nudged her clit. A zing of intensity sizzled through her. The ache at her nipples intensified.

She opened her mouth for more air and only managed a few harsh pants. The taps against her flesh grew harder, more intense. Verging on something more. He moved down one leg and up the other, until every inch of her tingled with sensation. Pressure built in her womb as the orgasm she craved more than her next breath grew imminent.

"That's good. Keep breathing." She barely heard his words over the buzzing in her ears. She did, however, notice the look in his eyes that gave her all the encouragement she needed. He was now her anchor as layer after layer of sensation built inside her. The thwaps of the crop grew more insistent, leaving a sharp sting in their wake. Still she kept her eyes on his and stayed the course, breathing in and out. It was hard to describe what she felt. It didn't really hurt. Every slap of leather gave her an odd mixture of both pain and pleasure that she could barely tell apart. Pressure intensified in her pussy in a rush every time the crop landed until she thought she might burst with the gathering desire.

He glanced down and another smile crossed his face. "So beautiful. Your little clit is standing at attention waiting for me to give it what it needs. But first…"

To her surprise, the taps from the crop ceased. "Oh…" She hoped this meant they were moving on to something a tad stronger. Like more of his hands or maybe his mouth. She whimpered just thinking about it.

"I don't know what you're thinking about, but I think I like it." He fiddled with the beads on the nipple clamps, eliciting a long moan from her. "But it's time to get these off."

Maggie whimpered, torn between the freedom

from the ever constant bite of the clamps and the ache of want still holding her tightly in its grasp.

Tucker leaned forward and kissed the upper slope of her right breast while his fingers made a quick path down her stomach to the small patch of hair between her legs. Before she could adjust to the new onslaught of sensations, he slipped his fingers between her wet folds and pressed two fingers inside her. With the palm of his hand applying constant pressure against her over-sensitized hot spot, Maggie went from zero to way past sixty in a matter of seconds.

Before her next breath he grasped a clip and removed the clamp from her left breast.

Maggie sucked in a sharp breath. Her vision wavered as pain flooded through her. She opened her mouth to speak and nothing came out. Frozen in this strange overwhelming sensation, her arousal ratcheted higher despite the pain.

"Breathe, Maggie. Your blood is rushing back to your nipple." His fingers moved inside her as he spoke. Impossible pressure built inside her.

Then he removed the second clamp and Maggie screamed loud and long. The sound hit her ears as dissociated from her body. Had it been she who screamed? She couldn't be sure. Her body raced to the edge of the cliff and hovered precariously.

Smiling, Tucker removed his hand and dropped the used clamps into a small sink she hadn't noticed before. Tears sprang to her eyes again and this time she couldn't hold them back. He was torturing her and that's all there was too it.

When he returned to her side she didn't bother trying to hide her face. He reached up and brushed a tear from her cheek. "You're so lovely like this. So much more than I expected." More tears slipped free and he continued to caress her cheek, catching each one.

She didn't know what to think. Her body demanded most of her attention. Between the gaze he'd locked with hers and the pulse of need that hammered through her, she was lost.

"Can I come down now?" Her confusion was ripping her up from the inside out. She didn't understand what he wanted from her at this point.

"No."

That was it. One word and no explanation. She wanted to yell in frustration.

He leaned over her shoulder to the frame of the wheel and unhooked it from the wall. "Besides being a beautiful backdrop for your portrait, this device does have other fun uses."

A sudden panic flashed through her. Fortunately he didn't make her wait long to discover what he meant. He grabbed the handle and began turning her torture trap. Spread-eagle and strapped to the metal, a sudden rush of air whistled between her legs. He stopped the contraption when he'd turned her completely upside down. She lifted her head and tried to see what he saw. With the angle of the device it proved too difficult to hold her head up and she relaxed back in position. So much for the blood rushing to her nipples. As if her mind wasn't foggy enough. Now she couldn't see beyond the bottom of the room and it didn't take a genius to know he now stared down at her open and available pussy.

"Now this is what I'm talking about." He opened another drawer and ripped into some packaging. Then his hands were on her pussy, slipping through the folds and spreading her lips wide. "Now I really get to play," he said.

Maggie shivered under the sudden onslaught that felt so good. Her eyes rolled back into her head. This had to be the strangest scenario she could have imagined. No control, a new fangled torture device and her in a position where he could and would do whatever he wanted to. And she couldn't care less. Any inhibitions she'd possessed had long slipped away.

Tucker opened her wider and blew on her clit at the same time some cool liquid spread across her opening. Her breath caught in her throat. Then he pushed something inside her. Something not his hands. Wide and firm. She squirmed. "Oh my God. What is that?"

"Be still. We don't have much time."

What?

She felt a pinch on her clit. And… Was that metal? Oh. My. God. He'd clamped her clit. Fresh streaks of pain splintered through her pussy and thighs. The almost-orgasm that had begun to fade came rushing forward. All at once everything throbbed. Her pussy, her nipples... Strangely, the extra blood to her head seemed to amplify everything. She had to come. Now.

Can't—Holy—uh—"

"Take deep breaths, Maggie. You're doing great." He squatted next to her and kissed a trail from her rib cage to each breast. The warmth of his touch calmed her. Gave her the chance she needed to catch her breath. The rising tension lowered a fraction.

He pulled back, slipped his finger in her mouth and hooked behind her lower teeth. "You're going to love this part."

He stood back up and a second later vibrations emanated from whatever he'd pressed inside her. She jerked and thrashed against her restraints. Her muscles inside and out tightened and flexed. The wheel began to move and she barely noticed until she was upright again and she stared into the watchful eyes of the man who continued to torture her with pleasure.

He reached between her legs and the vibrations sped up. Her eyes widened and he simply smiled. Moans one right after the other fell from her mouth and she squeezed her eyes closed.

"No, pet. Look at me. You will watch me when you come. I need that from you."

She couldn't. The sensations rocketed through her. Her stomach clenched, her muscles quivered and every inch of her skin tingled. A little more. Please God a little more. Her body was about to explode.

"Look at me." A sharp thwack landed on her thigh and her eyes sprung open. He stood in front of her, crop in hand, dark eyes flashing.

"You are amazing, Maggie." He swung the crop and another blow landed on her opposite thigh. Her back arched, reaching out for more. She was certain she was going to die any moment if she didn't get off.

"It's time, pet." Those simple words might have shot her from the wheel had she not been restrained. Her body bowed, so eager for anything and everything her Master wanted. Sweat rolled behind her neck and back as she strained for more.

"I wonder if this will make you scream."

There was no time to figure out what he meant. He removed the clamp from her clit and the sudden rush of blood coupled with the vibrations threw her violently off the edge she'd been perched on. Her mind splintered. Overwhelmed by the sheer force of pleasure, she fought the cuffs at her wrists and ankles like a wild banshee, thrashing from one side to the other. Her nerve endings burned in a relentless wave of sensation until her body collapsed.

Tucker grabbed her around the waist and

supported her weight. At his touch, more spasms rocked through her, sending her well into overdrive. Her muscles tensed, rendering her helpless to do anything other than feel each aftershock as it quaked through her. Draped across Tucker's chest, she lay there boneless as he worked to remove first the cuffs at her ankles and then her wrists.

Freed, she flopped forward until he scooped her into his arms and carried her across the room to the bed. Maggie barely registered any of his movements. Her brain was fried as she allowed him to lay her out on her back, grab a blanket and wrap her inside it before he lowered himself next to her and pulled her tight.

She allowed her eyes to drift closed and vaguely heard Tucker speaking to her. There was no comprehension, simply the haze she floated in. She had no idea how long she stayed like that. Days could have passed for all she knew. Her mind fluttered through the pleasure and intensity of Tucker until suddenly it re-fired.

Her eyes sprang open and the memories of her day flooded back to her in live action motion. Everything she'd allowed Tucker to do and then some. The hard band of his arm was wrapped around her waist leaving her afraid to move or breathe too heavily. What was he thinking? She'd behaved so—so out of control. Maggie fought not to wince and alert Tucker she'd recovered. Instead she inhaled deep and imprinted his delicious woodsy scent to memory. She wanted to remember him like this. Here in his art studio where he'd chosen to…

She couldn't finish the train of thought. Her stomach tightened. She had no choice but to move. Her clothes were on the other side of the house and her car even farther. She had to find the energy to not only get up, but escape his grasp.

Maggie wriggled in his arms to find he only tightened them around her more.

"Let me go, Tucker. I have to get up." He stirred behind her and the first thing she noticed was the hard-on pressed to her bottom. Oh my God, he didn't get off. The shock of that astounded her. Why had he stopped? Guilt flashed through her. Then another thought floored her. They weren't finished.

Maggie couldn't handle him right now. She'd lied. She wasn't ready. She fought harder against his hold and managed to loosen his grip. She sprang from the mattress and glanced around the room for something to cover her. When she found nothing she used her hands to cover her breasts and sprinted for the door.

"Maggie, what are you doing?"

She ignored him and kept going. She had to get out now. At the door, she turned back to him. "I'm sorry, Tucker. I have to go."

"Wait." He jumped from the bed and she didn't look back to see what he did. She ran the length of the covered walkway, found her clothes and grabbed them and then sprinted for the front door.

The bowl on the table held both her keys and his. She grabbed both sets.

"Maggie, I said wait. We need to talk about this."

Her steps faltered but she managed to keep going. The authoritative tone of his voice nearly compelled her to obey. She fought the compulsion to do as he asked. The almost incapacitating sensation of vulnerability started to slow her down, but her sense of self-preservation kept her in motion. She half-expected Tucker to catch her from behind and haul her back to his bed. Her stomach trembled at the thought. Even now, in flight, her doubts and needs warred side by side for dominance.

In the end, her head won out and she slipped through the door and made a beeline for her car. The fact that she was outside and completely nude gave her no pause. Fortunately Tucker lived on a private wooded estate that afforded him a ridiculous amount of privacy from a neighbor. She scrambled into her car and started it up. Without a look back, she gunned the gas and sped away from a house, or a homeowner, that now held a piece of her soul.

CHAPTER SIX

Tucker stood in his doorway and stared at the jagged tire tracks left behind in Maggie's wake. She'd bolted like a jackrabbit and caught him off guard. One minute he had his arms wrapped around the woman of his dreams and the next he'd watched her naked ass as she'd fled from his home before he could stop her.

He sighed and leaned his shoulder against the doorframe. She'd even grabbed his keys so he couldn't follow her. *Shit.* He hated the idea that she'd run out on him in the middle of an emotional overload. Anxiety and fear often came up at the end of an intense scene. He'd seen it in Maggie in spades. As if on cue, his painfully erect cock jerked against the front of his pants, reminding him of the condition Maggie's surrender had left him in. Not that he had any immediate plans to do anything about it.

No, as much as he'd wanted to sink into her warm, welcoming body they both needed more time. So much of the last few years for him had been a dark and dirty place. All the work he'd done to escape the nightmare of his youth had been a joke.

Fate was a cruel bitch and she'd made sure he had to come back home long before he was ready.

Tucker took a deep breath and shook off the old self-pity trying to worm its way back into his psyche. This past summer had been about healing, rebirth and second chances. At least he hoped so. Instead of mourning the loss of his future, or the sudden demands that came with inheriting an enormous tainted estate, he'd returned to the art he loved. Except for the weekly visits to see his mother at the mental hospital, he'd spent every hot day and waking minute in front of a burning furnace working everything out of his system with molten glass.

Hard physical labor and a love for the job became like a balm to the angry emotions that had driven him into the dark. Over time the rage and resentment had begun to fade and he'd had to work his way through the guilt and embarrassment for his behavior since his return.

Unfortunately this trip down memory lane wasn't doing him a damn bit of good when it came to one Maggie Cisco. He needed to find his spare keys and go after her. He had a duty to ensure her safety, both physical and mental. This wasn't the first time he'd seen a new submissive freak out after a scene but it was the first time someone had run out on him without even bothering to put on clothes.

A beep from his cell phone caught his attention. He scooped it up from the end table next to his couch and checked to see who was texting him.

I'm sorry I ran out like that but I need some time alone to think. Please don't follow me. Don't worry. I'm fine. Talk soon, Maggie.

Tucker drew his brows together and frowned at the phone. He didn't like the sound of this one bit. He understood all too well the need for space but not seeing her for himself did not sit well with him. Several minutes passed while he paced the room. He was ready to get in the car and go after her when the phone ringing in his hand caught him off guard. Automatically, he answered it without looking at the screen.

"Maggie?" he questioned.

"No, you bonehead this is not Maggie." He winced at his sister's voice. She did not sound happy with him. "What did you do?"

He was in no mood to get in a pissing contest with his sister over who knew what. Her moods pretty much changed with the wind and if he wasn't careful he'd get caught up in it.

"Hello to you, too."

"Don't even," she warned. "I'm serious as a fucking heart attack today. What the hell did you do?"

"Are we going to play twenty questions or can we just get to the point of what you think I've done?"

"Jesus, Tucker. You're such an ass sometimes."

He smiled. She had no idea. "And as usual, you

are as colorful as always my dear."

"Maggie's here."

Tucker straightened. "What? Why? Is she okay? Did she tell you what happened? Tell me."

"Whoa, whoa, whoa, big boy. I thought I was asking the questions. Don't even think about using your Jedi Dom mind tricks on me."

He sighed. One of these days someone was going to take Nina over their knee and make her learn the hard way not to be such a brat all the time. "Not in the mood, Nina. What's going on?"

"You really do suck the fun out of everything don't you. Fine. She showed up in the café about five minutes ago looking rather shell shocked. She took a table in the corner and with some prodding managed to order some coffee."

"Dammit. I'm on my way."

"Hold up, lover boy. If she looks like this because of something you did maybe you should give her some space to pull herself together. Why don't I talk to her? Feel her out first before you come crashing through here about as graceful as a bull in a china shop. Plus I've got your keys." He listened to her jangle them next to the phone.

"It's nice to know you think so highly of me. She did text me and ask for some time alone."

"Came on a little strong did you? Color me shocked."

"Your mouth is going to get you in a lot of

trouble some day. You really need to learn some manners."

Nina laughed. "Fuck that. Now tell me something I don't already know. Like what you did to make Maggie look so distressed. No wait. I have a feeling those details would require brain bleach to forget."

Tucker growled. Literally growled. His sister always found a way to get under his skin and drive him crazy. If he didn't love her…

"Look. Why don't you go back to your cave and do your artsy thing. I've got this and if I need you I'll let you know."

"I don't like this, Nina. If she's upset I need to be there."

"Tuck. Do the right thing here. Give the woman some damn space instead of smothering her to death. I WILL call you if you're needed."

His grip on the phone tightened as he fought every instinct to follow Maggie and bring her back. He couldn't wrap his mind around why she left in the first place so why wouldn't she want him to take care of her? It was his duty. His right.

"Helloooo. Are you listening to me?"

"Reluctantly," he answered.

"Are all you Dom types this stubborn?"

Tucker cringed. He already regretted telling his sister the truth about his past. His recovery might have required it but if she was going to bring it up all the time they'd have to have another talk.

"You don't really expect me to answer that do you?"

"Nope." Nina grunted and Tucker heard the sound of her feet hitting the floor. He imagined her sitting on her desk in her office behind the café, twirling the phone cord on the antique phone line she loved twice as much as her cell phone. "Later, Tuck. I'll call ya."

The phone disconnected and he stared at the screen. He brought the text back up from Maggie and started typing.

I want to help you. You don't have to be alone. But I'll honor your wishes, for now. Call me when you're ready.

Nina was right about one thing. He was dying to get back to the studio. Maggie had inspired him to start painting. His first love and primary source of stress relief would always be glass blowing, but with the frigid temperatures outside, it would be a while before he'd be working in front of the furnace again.

He'd puttered with some of his drawings for the last week, but it wasn't until he'd seen Maggie attached to the bondage wheel he'd finally been bit with the bug, again. Tucker returned to the studio and the first thing he noticed was the scent of Maggie and sex permeating the room. His groin tightened. The vivid memories of the beautiful sub restrained to his wheel slammed into him. He'd never seen a more beautiful wet and ready woman.

He took a seat in front of the canvas and began filling in some of the rough sketch. He focused on her eyes first. If he could capture all the emotions she shared with her expressions, the rest would come. He hunched closer and shaded first one and then the other. Right in front of him, Maggie came to life. His sweet, submissive pet. He'd captured the look in her eyes the moment she climaxed. Never in his life had he seen such perfect beauty as in that moment. From here on out he wanted to devote his life to making her come simply so he could watch and listen. Whatever it took, he'd do it just to witness the innocent, all-consuming pleasure of beautiful Maggie in the throes of her heart's desire.

Maggie gripped her cell phone and willed her hand to quit shaking. Relieved that Tucker wouldn't be coming through the door any minute, she tucked the phone into her pocket and stared into the coffee. She wasn't much of a java drinker but she loved the smell and the heat felt divine. Too bad her insides couldn't appreciate it.

As soon as she had cleared the sight line to Tucker's house she'd pulled over and hastily put on her clothing. It wouldn't do much for her already tattered reputation to get pulled over by some county cop for driving in the nude. Maggie laid her head down, pressing her forehead to the cool tabletop. She really was losing her mind.

Her thoughts had fractured in every direction the minute Tucker had told her to come and she'd never recovered. For someone who claimed to be an expert in the field of alternative lifestyles, she suddenly felt woefully inadequate to handle her own situation.

Minutes after she'd cleared the gates of the Lewis estate, she'd had to swallow her pride and admit she was in no condition to drive all the way home. Her legs were shaking and her heart pounded erratically. Her system was in overdrive and her thoughts were off the rails.

Tears burned at the back of her eyes. She sucked in a deep breath and willed them away. Things were bad enough without embarrassing herself in a public place. Especially one owned by Tucker's sister. Jesus hell. How had she escaped that information all these weeks? And of all the damn places to end up today of all days.

"Can I offer you a refill?

Speak of the devil.

"I'm good. Thanks." Maggie didn't lift her head. She couldn't face Nina at the moment.

"You don't look so good to me." Nina set the coffee pot down on the table and slid into the seat across from her.

She groaned inwardly. No. No. No. Small talk was not her forte to begin with. In her current state of mind it was totally out of the question.

Reluctantly, she lifted her head. "Look Nina, I

don't mean to be rude, but now is not the time for catch up. It's been kind of a rough day." Her breath hitched as she smothered a sob in her throat.

"Fair enough. Does it help to know that Tucker is worried about you?"

"Oh my God, seriously. He talked to you?" She had to get out of here. This was turning into the most embarrassing day of her life and that was saying something, considering the year she'd had.

"Maggie, don't look so horrified. I called him when you arrived. Honestly, the minute I saw you I knew something was wrong. Your eyes were glassy, your hair's a mess and your hands haven't stopped shaking since you came through my door."

"I'm—I don't—" Maggie took a deep breath and tried to think through what she wanted to say instead of the jumbled mess of nonsense that kept coming out of her mouth. "It's a pretty big leap from my being upset to assuming your brother is somehow involved."

Nina smiled. "Under normal circumstances sure. But I happened to be out back when you pulled in and saw what direction you came from." She covered Maggie's hand with her own. "There's only one thing in that direction for thirty miles."

The sound of rushing blood filled Maggie's ears. "I still don't want to talk about it." She might be acting like a two year old on the verge of a tantrum but there was a lot to be said for solitude around here. It's way too easy to forget how much everyone knew about everyone else in their small town. "Like I said to Tucker after I left, I need some space. In fact…" Maggie stood and grabbed her purse from the back of the chair. "I think it's time for me to head home. Thank you for the coffee."

"You're welcome." Nina stood as well. "I know I sound like a busy body trying to but into your business and all, but it's not how it's meant. I was truly concerned for you and am fully prepared to kick Tucker's ass for you if it comes to that. Brother or not, you say the word and I'll take him down a peg or two. God knows he needs it sometimes."

Shocked by Nina's words, Maggie stared dumbfounded. What was she supposed to say to that?

"I don't know the details about what happened, but I've always indulged in a hot bath and a glass of wine or three after a rough day. Tomorrow's bound to be better than today. Lord, I hope so."

Maggie barely smothered a giggle at Nina's strange southern charm. "How do you do that?"

Nina turned. "Do what?"

"Make it sound so easy."

The other woman scoffed. "Because it is that easy. Everyone has bad days and good days. And we all have our coping mechanisms, don't we?"

This time she couldn't stop the smile. Some of the rough edges of her psyche began to smooth. She'd forgotten how straight forward and in-your-face Nina tended to be. She dropped her purse at the base of her chair and plopped back into the seat. "Maybe you're right."

"Of course I am. Be sure to remind Tucker of that the next time you see him, I'd really appreciate it. He doesn't care much for my butting in to his business."

"I can't imagine why not."

They laughed together and Maggie felt more of her unease slip away. Maybe her decision to return home wasn't such a bad idea after all.

In the back of her mind, Maggie heard the front door chime and she stiffened. The woman in front of her transformed instantly. Her smile disappeared and her eyes widened. Nina's expression worried her and did nothing to ease Maggie's paranoia. In slow motion she turned to see who'd arrived while holding her breath. If Tucker had followed her, they were about to have words.

When she saw it was in fact not Tucker she almost sighed a breath of relief. But the big man looming in the doorway did not look happy. His intense stare in her direction forced Maggie to smother a gasp. She hastily turned in her seat and returned her attention to Nina. Although Nina paid no attention to Maggie. Instead, she sat transfixed on the gorgeous, if not a little scary, stranger, who had for all intents and purposes taken over the entire café with his presence.

"How about I make you some food? You can relax here as long as you want and I'll feel better knowing you've been taken care of. Deal?" Nina held out her hand in offering, and although she was speaking to Maggie, her eyes never left the man in the doorway.

"What's going on?" Maggie whispered to her friend. "Who is that man?"

For a second she didn't think the other woman had heard her.

"His name is Mason," Nina finally answered. "And he shouldn't be here."

Maggie tried not to laugh. Anyone not blind could see he mesmerized Nina. "Whatever you say. But when you come back down to earth, I'd like to hear all about it."

With obvious reluctance, Nina tore her gaze from the dark and scary, Mason. "Whatever you're thinking, it's not true. So, what do you say about that food?"

Maggie didn't hesitate. She didn't understand Nina's response, but wasn't about to miss this show. "Sure, why not?" Maggie replied.

"Soup sound good?"

"It sounds perfect, actually." Nina gave her a quick smile that didn't seem real and hustled in the direction of the kitchen. Relieved to have a brief distraction, Maggie relaxed, leaning her elbows on the table and resting her chin on her hands. She stared at the fire burning in the far corner and got lost in the movement of the flames as the wood popped and crackled in the space. Maybe stopping here had been fate. Nina had assured her that Tucker had agreed to give her the space she needed and once they got past the initial uncomfortable reunion, Nina had been very helpful.

A quick glance from the corner of her eye showed Mason had taken a seat not far from her. Out of hearing range, but it didn't take full audio to see this man tied her friend up in knots. Time passed and she eventually lost interest in the awkward discussion happening across the room. Nina's distraction gave Maggie the perfect opportunity to retreat into the solitude she'd been hoping for in the first place. Now if only she could get Tucker out of her head.

By the time Maggie got home, the sun had begun setting across the lake. With the barren winter trees surrounding the water, there were no barriers to the vivid colors from the sunset. Pinks, yellows and oranges striped the horizon as she drove the winding road to her parents cabin. She pulled to the edge of the road and got out. A slight breeze tugged at her bangs and sent a chill skittering down her spine. She zipped her jacket to just under her chin and crossed her arms to ward off the cold already settling in.

The frosty air didn't deter her from getting some fresh air. The beauty of the lake was hard to resist in any season but she especially loved the winter. It was the restful period of the year before the busy season of spring began. Once the water warmed and the plants began to grow the lake got overrun by enthusiastic boaters and an influx of tourists and college students. On an evening like this she wasn't likely to run into anyone, which is exactly the way she wanted it.

There was so much to ponder. Her knowledge for one. Over the years she'd been meticulous about her research, taking care to document all of her findings in painstaking detail. All for nothing. Intellectual knowledge of BDSM simply did not compare to intimate knowledge. Tucker had made that clear.

Maggie shoved her hands in her hair and sighed loudly. Her frustration over this ran deep and she didn't know how to reconcile who she'd been this morning with who she was now.

Not that she had any idea what the hell that meant. "Fuck!" She yelled the word at the top of her lungs.

She had half a mind to go straight to her office and start deleting half her life's work. It was all like one colossal fraud. As if she'd been pretending all along to understand something she knew little about. Kind of like how she felt when she was a young girl and she dressed in her mother's clothes and play-acted what it would be like to be a doctor. She listened to her parents discuss medicine and then she'd take that knowledge to play her role. Is that what she'd done all her life? A role? First her job, then her marriage and then her research.

Maggie lifted her head. What about the book she was writing? Her outlook perked up. Maybe she could use her experience to enrich her research instead of negating it. She'd have to start over with fresh eyes and come at it from a different perspective. Excited to have an idea, she hurried back to her car. She desperately wanted to get to her computer and her notes so she could start making changes. Idea after idea flew through her mind. Ducking into her car, she grinned. The breakthrough she'd been hoping for all along had hit her like a ton of bricks and she owed it all to Tucker.

Maybe when she finished her book, she'd reconsider his offer. Maggie closed the car door and shoved the key in the ignition. For now, she only wanted her computer and maybe a few gallons of caffeine. She had a new story to tell.

CHAPTER SEVEN

Tucker blinked and stared at the canvas in front of him. How long had he been sitting here? The quick sketch he'd done of Maggie on the bondage wheel had been transformed into a painting almost as lush as the woman herself. The stark nature of the wood and steel contrasted sharply with the creamy expanse of her skin. Although the memory of the real thing far outweighed any picture.

He moved his neck from side to side and rolled his shoulders. There were no clocks in the studio but his body told him he'd worked way beyond normal as did the finished artwork. Normally a painting of half this caliber would take him weeks. Not days.

Days. Holy shit. He'd worked, slept and ate without leaving this room for at least a few days. He glanced at the cell phone plugged into the wall on the bedside stand. And not a single call since he'd spoken to his sister the day Maggie fled.

Maggie's silence worried him. It had been a bone-headed move on his part to let things go this long. A mistake he would rectify no matter what it took. While he'd worked at a feverish pace on his masterpiece, he'd relived the scene they enjoyed together over and over again, trying to pinpoint at what moment it had gone wrong. Nothing stuck out to him. She'd reacted to every demand like a natural, her body singing to him the farther he took her. It wasn't until after, when the adrenaline began to crash that her brain had probably kicked in.

He hated to think what thoughts had prompted her to run, but he'd been a Dom long enough to know that a new sub could and likely would crash pretty hard. If he hadn't been so concerned for her well-being, the site of her streaking naked out his front door would have made him laugh. For her sake, he was grateful he'd given the housekeeper the day off.

Tucker stood and moved to the desk where he did all of his non-artistic work and booted up his computer. He punched in a password and pulled up the file he'd compiled on everything he could find about Maggie since she'd graduated high school and left town. She'd finished college at the top of her class and immediately took a position teaching at her alma matter where she'd begun dating a fellow professor shortly after she started her new job. Soon after, she wrote her first paper on BDSM and was granted funding to continue her research into the effects of the alternative lifestyle on a long-term basis.

One year later, she married her professor boyfriend and after that the only information he could find was purely professional. Not a single detail about her personal life had been published that he could dig up. Until she'd been arrested... Then there'd been some rumors about her sex life, more than a few jokes published at her expense, and even an article questioning her ability to teach young adults. Something still nagged at him, though. He'd dismissed most of what he'd read as normal tabloid trash, but the look in her eyes in one of the photographs gave him pause, he couldn't get her out of his mind.

"What other secrets do you have in your closet, Miss Maggie?" He flipped to the picture that had been featured on the front page of the college newspaper. Maggie, dressed in typically conservative clothes being hauled out of a very well known BDSM club in handcuffs. From there things went downhill fast. Thanks to a highly publicized interview between Maggie and the author of a new bestselling erotic thriller, the journalists had begun suggesting that Ms. Cisco had been attempting to turn a fictional novel into a real life scenario between her and two of the patrons of the club.

Tucker turned away from the screen when the pain in his temple began to throb. He understood bad timing all too well and Maggie had it in spades. He pushed away from the desk and scooped up his phone. He flipped the screen to Maggie's number and clicked new message.

It was time for them both to move forward. This

time he'd try a different approach. He'd start a trail to lead her to him one step at a time. This time he'd make sure she got everything she needed without letting her go. He quickly typed a few words and pressed send. Time to get a shower and get some fresh air. He had a sub to go after.

Again.

The annoying ring tone of an incoming text message startled Maggie from her manuscript. Or more precisely her latest journal entry about her and Tucker. Why had she left the cursed thing on? She scooped the phone from her desk and stared at the screen.

We need to talk.

Maggie's heart skipped a beat and she glanced around the café she'd escaped to, to make sure he wasn't already watching her. She'd known this moment was coming for three days and had dreaded it as much as she'd questioned why she hadn't heard from him. Her thoughts had ranged from nonchalance to complete irrationality. She still had no idea what to say or do. She'd tried over and over to restart her new biography to only keep erasing everything she wrote. The whole project was crumbling before he eyes. Finally, she'd set it aside and started a personal journal instead. Getting some of what she'd endured these past few months onto paper had led to not much sleep and a whole lot of pouring her heart out.

Now she sat exhausted, staring at the phone in her hand. Unsure. Maybe even as confused as ever. She looked up and stared through the window to the trees outside. What time was it anyway? She'd lost track. Not that it made a difference. The beauty of coming here in the first place was that there would be no schedules to adhere to. No lies to live. And certainly no one to answer to.

Unless she counted Tucker.

She sighed and leaned back in her chair. Tucker had come to her out of the blue and shocked the hell out of her. Initially she'd been shaken to the core of her beliefs, but as she'd spent more time analyzing what had happened, her reaction to him had softened. It was kind of humiliating that she'd run away, but at the time, it had been all the logic she'd been capable of. In one scene, he'd twisted her inside out and upside down.

Her research still plagued her, but regrets no longer did. Everything up to now had led her to Tucker and who was she to discount fate for dropping him in her path on a cold winter's night?

She slid her phone apart to reveal the keyboard and tapped out a return message.

I owe you an apology.

Her stomach tensed. There were a lot of creative ways for a Dominant to accept something as simple as an apology. She didn't know whether to be scared or excited. It could easily go either way. Maybe if they talked first, she could explain some of what had been going through her head these past few days. There was a lot he didn't know. Hell, there was a lot nobody knew. Some of which continued to eat her up inside. Somehow, someway, she needed to get it out if she ever hoped to put the past behind her.

For years she'd done what everyone else expected of her. Went to the right schools, took the right job and married respectably. The only thing in her life she'd taken a stand on had been her research. And the first time she stepped out of line, everything she'd built fell apart, leaving her with an unknown future. Her missteps had the tendency to leave her without the courage to face up to her mistakes. Maggie rolled her eyes. She needed to stop making so many damned excuses and just get on with it already. Maybe if she stopped worrying about every little detail she'd find if she and Tucker suited each other.

What a joke. The fallen prince and his scandalous woman. What a pair they'd make. The internet had become her friend these last few days as she researched for her book and the man who made her tremble. Much of what she'd read left her shocked about how clueless she'd been. Since her parents had moved from the area after she left for college, she'd never bothered to keep up with the local news, or any news that didn't relate to her research, for that matter. She hadn't exactly forgotten that Tucker's father led a fringe religious group. But a cult? That had taken quite a while to digest.

Her phone beeped again.

Have dinner with me tonight. We'll go out this time.

Such a benign request after the way they'd left things. A sliver of disappointment knifed through her before her brain kicked in. If she really wanted to have a discussion, dinner in a public restaurant sounded perfectly reasonable. Too bad her body couldn't get on the same page as her brain. It was crazy hard not to think about the clever way he'd manipulated her body over and over until her head damn near exploded.

Before she could type out a response, her phone beeped.

My driver will pick you up at seven. Expect a package this afternoon. Follow all of the instructions. ALL of them.

This time her stomach flipped and tumbled. She read his words on her phone, but had heard the command in her head. Almost felt his breath at her ear.

"Whatcha doing?" Nina dropped into the seat across from Maggie and craned her head to get a look at Maggie's phone.

A hot flush rushed up Maggie's head and neck. Busted. "Nothing." She closed her phone and prayed she hadn't done something to embarrass herself.

"If that's nothing, can I have some? I don't think I've seen anyone glow from nothing."

Good lord. She looked down at the table and hoped for some giant mysterious sinkhole to open and swallow her now before Nina grilled her to death. "You're crazy, you know that?"

Her friend snorted. "We may not have seen each other in a bazillion years but I can still tell when you're lying. I can tell when anyone is. It's a gift, you know."

Perhaps Maggie didn't know for certain how to handle what happened between her and Tucker or what her future might hold, but the minute she and Nina had reconnected they might as well have been teenagers again. It had happened so quickly and naturally she didn't understand how they'd managed to avoid each other through most of high school.

"And you're too nosy for your own good." She closed her laptop and packed it away in her carrying case. "I need to head home."

"Why's that? Got a hot date?"

Maggie gaped at Nina.

Nina stared at her for a beat before she broke out into hysterical laughter. "Oh my God. Why couldn't I have captured that face with my cell camera? So priceless." She laughed harder until she grabbed her stomach and tears came to her eyes.

"I'm not even going to pretend I know what you find so funny. You've gotten really weird in your old age."

"If you didn't look like I'd just caught you

stealing or something it probably wouldn't be so funny. I take it you finally heard from my wayward brother."

She nodded.

"What did he have to say for himself?"

Maggie squirmed in her seat. The last thing she wanted to do right now was go over this with Nina.

Nina compressed her lips and curled them in, making it obvious she was trying to hide a smile.

Maggie leaned in. "You know, one of these days someone is going to come along and wipe that smug smile off your face. They are going to twist you up inside and make you want to do things you've never considered. Then I'll be the one across the table laughing." She grabbed her purse and slung it over her shoulder as she stood to leave.

"Aww, don't go away mad." Her friend smiled as the words left her mouth.

Maggie smiled back at her. "You're a brat."

Nina stood and walked her to the door. "It's that very brattiness that keeps my friends coming back for me. You're all gluttons for punishment."

"If you say so." Maggie opened the door and strode through it. Before it closed behind her she heard parting words from Tucker's sister.

"See you tomorrow. Same bat time. Same bat channel."

She laughed out loud as she made her way to her car. It truly was impossible not to leave Nina with a smile on her face. The woman had a knack for turning any bad mood around by reminding people to enjoy the little things. A hot cup of coffee, a cupcake, and most importantly, a laugh.

*

Not ten minutes after Maggie walked through her front door. The doorbell rang. She hustled to answer it, excitement buzzing through her blood. She couldn't wait to see what Tucker had sent.

As soon as she opened the door, the delivery guy shoved a huge white box into her arms.

"I need you to sign here." He produced a clipboard and a pen from under his arm and shoved it in her face.

Too excited to think, Maggie grabbed the board, scribbled her name and thrust it back to the man. She was dying to open the box. With a quick kick of her leg, she closed the door and rushed to her bedroom. There might not be anyone else staying in the house with her, but she needed the privacy of her own room before she opened her present.

In her head, she knew she should savor this moment by slowly unwrapping the package one layer at a time. In reality, she tore into the box and accompanying white tissue like a little kid who stayed awake all night waiting for Christmas morning to arrive.

Inside, she found luxurious silk pooled seductively among the wrappings. She gingerly lifted the garment from its container and admired the gorgeous dress Tucker had sent. The shimmering gold color of the fabric reminded her of champagne and the crystals sewn in to the bodice of the halter even resembled the bubbles. She rubbed the luxurious material against her cheek and sighed. It didn't take much to imagine how the fabric would cup her breasts and the delicate pleats at the waist would drape the skirt perfectly across her curves. The decadence of it overwhelmed her.

Then her eyes caught the shoebox tucked into the corner of the package. She set aside the dress and lifted the top. She gasped again at what lay inside. She might not own a single pair of Christian Louboutin shoes, but every woman recognized the familiar red soles that were the designer's trademark.

Oh God.

She couldn't contain her excitement. In two seconds flat, she'd removed her cute and far more practical leather boots and slid the first beige patent pump on her right foot. What could have been considered ordinary were turned extraordinary by four inch heels that she knew would make her legs look long and sleek. Of course they fit perfectly. How did he—?

Maggie shook her head. Probably his sneaky half sister. She'd not seemed all that surprised about Tucker contacting her today or by her sudden departure. In fact, she probably already knew every detail about her upcoming date. She cocked her head. No problem, two could play at that game.

She slipped out of the shoes and placed them back in the box. Part of her wanted to refuse such expensive gifts from Tucker and the other wanted to embrace anything and everything about what lay ahead. It was difficult not to conjure the look on Tucker's face as she'd been tied to his bondage wheel. It was the first time any man had looked at her like that. As if he would burn alive with desire if he didn't have her right that second.

Her sex squeezed, reminding her how empty she'd felt these last few days without him. He'd given her a taste of what submission could mean for her and she really wanted more. Although she'd had to remind herself on every occasion that it wasn't normal to obsess over a man she barely knew.

Maggie fell on the bed and stared at the pink chandelier she'd loved as a teen. High school had been kind of weird for her. She'd clung to her then boyfriend until he sort of broke her heart. For a while she'd thought she loved him, then she'd kissed Tucker that fateful spring night at a carnival, leaving her little teenaged heart more confused than ever. Not that she'd done anything about it. Good girls didn't rock the boat or dump their popular football player boyfriends. She scrunched her face. From the unexplained attraction to Tucker at a young age to a loveless marriage and the research that served as an excuse to learn about something she craved on a basic level but had no intention of pursuing beyond a toe in the water. So far she'd managed to live her life in a bubble. Not that she hadn't burst it in a big, ridiculous way.

Stop. Don't do this.

This was no time to revel in her stupid, stupid mistakes. Lesson learned thank you very much. Now she only had to take a shower, shave all her important girl parts and don a dress to go meet a boy. A boy that had grown up to be so much more than she expected. Her stomach fluttered again. She jumped from the bed and stripped down to nothing. Last time she'd gone to Tucker she'd completely freaked out. Tonight, she'd go in with her eyes wide open and her expectations high. She had a fantasy and only one man could fulfill it.

CHAPTER EIGHT

Tucker drummed his fingers on the wooden bar while keeping his eyes on the entrance. Any moment now Maggie would walk through those doors and the night of decadence he'd planned for her would begin. He'd decided he needed to go big or go home. He'd gone big.

He looked forward to bringing Maggie farther into his world and watching her reaction. Tonight she'd learn more about him than he revealed to anyone. There were a few secrets he'd kept to himself. Not because he was afraid or ashamed of the life he'd built. But there were some things so spectacular that he selfishly refused to share them with the world.

Part of him wanted to treat Maggie like that. Wrap her up and keep her hidden from curious onlookers and any potential reporters on her tail. Once they got the scent of a relationship, they'd be on them both like a shark to blood. Her recent troubles were bound to be splashed across newspapers and gossip rags larger than the first go round thanks to the world's incessant interest in

BDSM this past year. Add some money to the story and things got much worse. He hoped she understood what getting involved with him entailed. Maybe that's the talk they needed to have first. From shunned son of a suspected cult leader to billionaire sex addicted playboy, he'd attracted more than his fair share of attention over the years.

Fortunately, he didn't interest many reporters these days other than the local paper. When he wasn't ensconced in his art studio working around the clock, he'd come out just long enough to pick a fight with the town council over some asinine issue or another. On one level, small town life suited him very well. No corporate pressure to be something he wasn't and for the most part people left him alone. He imagined he still managed to be a regular mention in the gossip mill, but as long as he didn't hear about it, he could care less.

Let them talk. Let them wonder why a man his age preferred his own company over others. Well, until now. Maggie's arrival back in town had caused a shift in him. She reminded him that there was more to life than creating art and aggravating city forbearers that were forced to deal with him because he'd inherited his father's position on their council. He smirked. No democracy in this town. The only way a member got in or out was through death.

From the beginning, he'd toed the line to an extent. While not his nature under normal circumstances to go with the flow, he simply had no interest in deciding what businesses had to be shut down or how to deal with particularly embarrassing residents. It did however, serve as a reminder of exactly how conservative his father had been in the public eye. No one had ever known exactly what George Lewis had been capable of in his private life until the very end.

Disgusted by his train of thought, Tucker slid the glass of alcohol away and turned to observe the room. It was amazing what a difference a thirty-minute ride from home did to your surroundings. He recognized a few people scattered among the dining tables but for the most part he faced a sea of strangers. How many knew they were sitting in a façade? Would they be shocked to know they were only separated by a few soundproofed walls from the kinkiest sex club in the city?

Purgatory wasn't exactly a secret. Thanks to the occasional protestors, the goth fetish club he co-owned managed quite a bit of public scrutiny.

"Wow. Twice in one week. Are you going for a new record this year, boss?"

Tucker didn't need to turn his head to recognize his club manager, Gabe. He and his equally private business partners had long ago relinquished the day-to-day operations of the club to this man, preferring to keep their names out of the press and ensure the club ran smoothly without them.

"For some reason you are not the first person to be shocked by my appearance."

Gabe laughed and the two shook hands. "Have you come to partake of a friendly submissive this evening? We have several available that I think would serve you well."

"What's with everyone trying to offer me a sub? Do I have a look of desperation I'm not aware of?"

Gabe didn't even react to that statement. "So you've decided it's time to take a more active role in the management of Purgatory, then."

"Jesus hell, Gabe. Lighten up. I have a date. Is that so hard to believe? Besides, you know as well as I do how much my privacy means to me. The last thing I need right now is for any local reporters butting into any of my business. I've got enough to worry about these days…"

The other man's shoulders relaxed a fraction. Tucker puzzled over what had Gabe so on edge. The man had a reputation for complete and utter control over any situation, but tonight something bothered him. When he was about to open his mouth and get to the bottom of the situation, something caught Gabe's attention and he turned to the front door.

"I'd offer to buy you a drink but I have a feeling the reason you're here has just arrived."

Tucker checked his watch before he turned and smiled. Right on time. He swiveled in the direction of the door and immediately felt all the blood from his head drain to another very important part of his anatomy. His vision narrowed as he focused entirely on the woman standing at the entrance of the restaurant. With her skin slightly flushed and her top teeth nibbling at her lower lip she made all the things he wanted to do to her jump into his brain at once.

She'd honored him by wearing the outfit he'd provided and she looked gorgeous. Despite his original intentions, he'd opted for something a bit more high class than typical dungeon wear. Then his gaze caught site of the shoes. He bit back a groan. He'd always had a nut for fuck me heels, but on Maggie, fuck me took on a whole new meaning. More like bend me over, plow my ass and have your way.

She spoke to the hostess for a moment, giving him a little more time to seek control. He had half a mind to skip dinner and go straight to the evening's entertainment. He wanted her in the dungeon now. Small talk and romance could wait.

She followed the direction the hostess pointed and their gazes finally met. The jolt in his groin made him grateful he still sat at the bar. He wasn't sure his legs could work under the intensity of that single look. It was one of the things he loved most about her. The expressive eyes. All of her emotions stood plainly visible at any given moment. Even after everything she'd been through lately, there was an air of seductive innocence cloaking her. She'd taken her hits and moved on. Except for the death grip she had on her purse, she managed to look the epitome of calm.

Relieved that he still set her a little off balance, Tucker slid from his stool at the bar. Without taking his eyes from Maggie he spoke to Gabe, "We should have a meeting soon."

"Sure thing, boss. How about I call you in a couple of days to set something up."

Tucker nodded and moved to greet the sexy woman coming his way.

"Hi," she spoke first, the single word breathless.

"Hi yourself."

Her lips parted, and a lovely smile crossed her face. For a breathless moment he waited before he cupped her head, drew her close and covered her mouth with his. He swallowed the small sigh that fell from her mouth as the pleasure of having her in his arms again sank into his bones. The sensation of her soft body against the hard planes of his reminded him what he'd been missing these last several days. He nearly groaned.

He threaded his fingers through her hair and tugged her a notch closer. They might have been in the middle of a public restaurant but he knew very few of the patrons would be shocked by his behavior. Tucker took advantage of her surprise and swept his tongue between her parted lips. Soft heat filled his senses as he tasted and explored every inch. She grabbed his arms and wrapped her fingers around his biceps. It wouldn't take much to make her forget they had an audience.

Slowly, he stepped back when all he wanted to

do was grab her hand and lead her to Purgatory. All doubts about Maggie and where she belonged evaporated. He'd been without a submissive for a very long time and she possessed the perfect amount of desire to submit mixed with stubborn female fight to keep things interesting. As long as he didn't push her too far too fast again. This time he'd hold her to him and there'd be no running tonight.

The image of her fleeing from his house naked had him biting back a smile. No way would he ever regret that memory as long as he lived. It had been a sight to behold. The combination of frightened rabbit and ivory female skin still flushed from orgasm. He sighed. She'd dumbfounded him until he started painting.

"I've missed you," he blurted, cupping her chin and rubbing his thumb along her bottom lip.

"I missed you too," she confessed. "I feel like an idiot the way I ran out the other day."

He pressed his finger to her lips. "Shh. We'll work through that later. Did you find my special gift and the instructions for it?"

She nodded, her eyes dropping to the floor.

His brow raised and his eyes narrowed a fraction. "I didn't hear you" he stated.

Her eyes widened when she realized what he expected. She cleared her throat before she spoke, "Yes, Sir."

"Good girl. We're going to have a very good time tonight. But for now I'd like to have dinner.

Would you care to join me?"

"Yes, please," she answered, her voice coming out huskier than she'd probably expected. Him bringing up his little surprise placed them squarely back into their Dominant/submissive roles. Her demeanor changed as did her breathing. Damn. The thought of her taking the small tube of lube he'd provided and preparing her little asshole for a plug stirred his cock. He'd seriously considered making her bring it to the restaurant for him to place the first time. It would have been simple to slip into one of the private changing rooms and push the pretty pink toy between her sweet checks.

Tucker's entire body hardened. He'd never make it through a normal dinner at this rate. His intention for having her prepare her body for him was a two-fold decision. First, she'd have to make the decision to follow his request or not, all on her own without any pressure from him in person. And second, it pleased him to have a submissive take the time to prepare her body for his pleasure. While he had every intention of giving her more pleasure than she'd dreamed of, she would have to work for it. Earn it per se. He'd taken this opportunity as a test to see how willingly she accepted his commands after the mishap of their previous encounter.

Of course, now all he thought about was what that little plug did to her. Before long she'd be squirming in her seat. Tucker forced back his reaction and smiled as he led them away from the bar. He'd chosen the perfect spot for their dinner.

Fire and Ice had been designed to be different from a sea of restaurant choices in Charlotte. The front dining room was all about ice, with a series of cascading waterfalls that fell into pools filled with rocks that looked like chunks of ice. Farther back they'd chosen to embrace the fire. Levi had designed the walk in sized fireplace that dominated the space with flames so high they looked capable of reaching forward and licking the skin of anyone that got too close.

The semi-private booth he'd reserved served as the perfect backdrop for a meal. With the curved wall around the back of the booth, they'd be blocked from the view of the vanilla customers while still allowing them to see and be seen by the diners that utilized the full spectrum of services at dinner. He couldn't wait to see the look on her face if something happened while she nibbled on her appetizer. Actually, he was counting on it.

When they reached their table, Tucker motioned for her to slide in first. She carefully sat and gently slid along the smooth leather. Oh yeah, she was feeling it. He took the spot next to her, sitting so close that their thighs touched. He leaned in and placed his lips next to her ear. "How are you feeling now, pet?"

She twisted her hands together and then placed them palms down on the table in front of her. "Excited…Uncomfortable…Nervous," she replied.

"You look amazing. I enjoy the flush of your skin when you're aroused." He'd spoken the words a little louder this time, catching her off guard.

"I'm not—"

She'd been about to lie to him and stopped. "Very good girl." He squeezed her leg, "we've already got some punishment time to work through later. I doubt you want to add anymore by lying to me."

Maggie squirmed in her seat, her thigh rubbing against his.

"What am I being punished for?" Her voice shook a bit as she spoke, but it was the husky undertone that spiked his attention. His body automatically responded to the sound of her arousal. *Oh Miss Maggie. We are in so much trouble.*

"While I understand how overwhelmed you must have been the other day to run away, that kind of behavior is not acceptable. If you have any kind of problem with what's going on between us, it's my job to make adjustments as necessary. Running around town with your head out of sorts can be extremely dangerous. I'm sure you've heard of aftercare. If you hadn't found your way to my sister, I would have followed you and probably dragged you back to my house and then paddled you until you couldn't sit."

Maggie gulped. "I'm sorry, Tucker. I feel so stupid about my behavior. I don't know what got into me."

He covered her hand with his. "Never be sorry for how you feel, little one. I only care that you tell me so we can deal with it. Without the ability to communicate, we'll get nowhere fast. Do you think you can handle that?"

"Yes, Sir," she responded.

Tucker's stomach tightened. To hear *Sir* from her lips unprompted fired his blood. "Good. Of course that doesn't take away the punishment you have coming, but it leaves us free to move on in our conversations." He smiled and motioned to the waiter to come forward from where he'd hovered, to take their order.

Tonight would make or break their future together. As he led her deeper into his private world, they'd both find out whether their long-term desires were compatible. He suspected she'd enjoy every minute of what he wanted her to experience even if it took her way outside her comfort zone. She'd somewhat proven that the other day. Their scene had been blunt and intense. He still got hard every time her thought of her soft cries and the flood of wetness that greeted him between her thighs. She'd loved every minute of it, until she crashed.

He planned to repeat the effect of their previous encounter without letting her freak out afterward. With proper aftercare she'd be like putty in his hands. He couldn't wait.

The waiter went through the specials and he sat back and observed Maggie as she chose what she wanted to eat and drink. There were a million and one little things about her that he continued to enjoy. The light in her eyes when she talked about something she cared about. Or the attention to detail she conveyed in the papers she'd written on the BDSM lifestyle. She never got the facts wrong but there was enough of a hesitant undertone in her findings to indicate that she wrote from research and not experience. He looked forward to the change after tonight.

The waiter took her menu and left them alone.

"You're not eating?" she asked.

"Of course I am. But I've been here enough the staff knows what to bring me without having to ask."

"Wow. I've never heard of this place. Although that doesn't mean anything since I've been away so long," she qualified. "There are probably a lot of changes I know nothing about."

Tucker used her last statement as the segue he needed to steer the conversation. "How long has it been since you've been home?"

Maggie's demeanor changed. Her back stiffened, her eyes shuttered, even the rest of her body seemed to curl in on itself as if she needed to protect herself. That would not do. Tucker wrapped his arm around her shoulder and threaded his fingers through the hair at her neck. She was so different from the women he'd been with. Where they had long flowing locks that he wrapped around his hands, Maggie kept her hair much shorter than most women with layers that made the edges look a bit spiky. The style flattered her very well and to him it was a nice change from the fake bottle blondes he'd gotten used to.

The same thing with her body. There was nothing fake about Maggie Cisco. He slid his hands from her neck along the curve of her spine. He'd specifically chosen this dress because of the skin lines it left open to him. As an artist he did everything with his hands, and when it came to women he was often the same way. Right now he itched to stroke and pet every inch of the beautiful submissive sitting next to him.

She still hadn't answered him but he felt her muscles relaxing under his ministrations. He wasn't in a hurry tonight and he had enough patience to wait for her answer. For now.

"Until last month, I hadn't been here since I graduated from college."

Tucker calculated the math in his head, estimating how long it had taken her to get her Master's and half of her Doctorate degree. Ten years almost. He softly whistled. That was a long damn time to stay away.

"Why so long?"

She shrugged like it didn't matter but he'd learned to read a woman's body language and the answer filled her with tension.

"My parents didn't care much for my ex."

Curious. His research into her ex husband hadn't netted a whole lot to get excited about. Kyle Dixon. With a moniker as exciting as milk toast, he'd matched his name to a T. Fifteen years older than Maggie, he'd been forty when they got married.

"Why's that?" he coaxed. Maybe there was more to her story than he'd realized.

She shrugged again. "At first he was too old for me. Then he'd been too stuck up for them. Over the years the reasons why increased and I stopped listening. They stopped in to see me every time they left for another poverty-stricken country to save the world, which was often, so there wasn't much need to make the trek here. The cabin is pretty much empty year round now."

That part he'd known. Her parents were well-known for their minimalistic living style and high ideals. Most people called them hippies who happened to have medical degrees.

"You must have disagreed with their assessment." He felt like he was entering dangerous territory. It served neither of them to go wandering around in the past. Especially his.

She nodded her head. "For a while. Then we grew apart and the little things started to matter. He hated my research." The sadness in her voice annoyed him. He didn't want her dwelling on the past when they had such potential for a future.

"You have a beautiful mind, Maggie. I've read many of your papers and was impressed."

Her head swiveled sharply. "You've read my papers?"

Tucker smiled. "Of course I did, pet. How else would I learn about what my new submissive might have been thinking when she fled the scene."

"Your submissive?" her voice lowered to a whisper again. "I thought this was just an experiment for me and I don't know.. just sex for you?"

"I've thought about you a lot these last few days and I have no interest in a fuck and run. I relish the idea of exploring your knowledge and its practical application. You're a smart, fascinating woman with a strong history of independence." Of course, he'd have to keep her close and watch her like a hawk. He'd started this journey and it was his job to keep her safe. "Call me smitten."

CHAPTER NINE

Maggie tried to swallow past the sudden lump in her throat. *His submissive.* She hadn't processed much beyond those two words. Blood rushed to her head as she tried to make sense of this new direction. Never in her wildest dreams had she thought... Well, maybe in her wildest dreams. But c'mon, her and Tucker? So far she'd lived up to every one of Kyle's accusations. A repressed, uptight know-it-all who thinks just because she researches BDSM that she's smarter about sex than everyone else.

Some of the repressed anger that Maggie had survived on began to flood through her. Kyle could go fuck himself. They were divorced now and she was under no obligation to keep his precious secrets. This was her new life and she deserved to live it, whatever that turned out to be. She forced her old stupid self out of the way and focused on the unbelievably hot man in front of her.

"What do you expect from a submissive?" she asked. Was this what he considered average conversation at dinner? Maggie bit her lip to keep from smiling. She didn't know what Tucker had in mind for her, but there was no need to make it worse by laughing at him.

"A lot of it is probably what you're already thinking. I won't lie and tell you its not very sexual for me. A woman who submits to me of her own free will, with an open mind, drives me crazy. It's the perfect gift." His fingers continued to stroke her spine from the base of her neck to the top of her ass. The more he touched the more she reacted. She was aware of the plug inside her more than ever. It didn't hurt. Quite the contrary. Every time she squirmed in her seat or his fingers sent a shudder coursing through her, the toy touched some sort of nerve ending and reawakened it.

"I especially love doing anything and every thing to torture with pleasure. You are probably experiencing some of that now."

She blew out a hard breath. "You have no idea."

"Actually I do. When I got interested in the lifestyle I went to a very thorough trainer."

He left it at that and Maggie whimpered. What a tease. She wanted to know details. If she pictured him with… Oh God.

"While most of my interest lies in dominating you sexually, I live my life very much in control, so I'll probably take charge a lot. While I do love a good spanking, if I have to get more creative with my punishments, I'm up for the challenge. Have you ever heard of domestic discipline?"

Her stomach tumbled as more excitement built. "Yes, of course."

"We'll set up rules and breaking them will always come with consequences. Especially if it in any way jeopardizes your safety."

She watched him intently as he explained his expectations. She loved the clear excitement shining in his eyes. She'd never experienced this level of communication with a lover and it felt refreshing.

Though Tucker wasn't technically her lover yet. What did she call a man who'd tied her to a bondage wheel and touched her more intimately than anyone before without actually having sex? He'd gone without pleasure throughout their entire scene, yet he sat next to her explaining how she would become his submissive.

Talk about surreal.

"How do you feel so far? Okay?"

Maggie blinked, tuning into Tucker's voice. "Yes, Sir," she answered without hesitation.

"Good, because there is more. Some of which you will discover tonight."

Her muscles clenched. She had a feeling whatever he had up his sleeve for the rest of their date was going to blow her mind.

"I've been known to share my submissive."

"Really?" she blurted. He couldn't have shocked her more if he'd tried although why she couldn't say. There were so many facets to BDSM and sharing was not at all uncommon. Some of her old fantasies resurfaced.

"I wondered how you'd react to that little nugget. Although I'm not sure you understand what I'm saying."

Maggie creased her brow. "What do you mean?"

"My kink has its limits. Most of the time, we'll be alone out at the house, where things can be as casual or as strict as I like. But every once in a blue moon I like to go to a club and all that entails. Protocols, leather, intense equipment and sometimes playing with others."

"More intense than a bondage wheel?"

Tucker grabbed a fistful of her hair and slowly pulled her neck back. "Stop interrupting, Miss Maggie. You don't want to borrow more trouble than your butt can cash tonight."

A giggle slipped from her mouth. She couldn't help herself. "I haven't heard anyone say that since I was a little girl and my mother was getting annoyed with me."

His grip on her hair tightened and the pleasure sensation of his dominance edged closer to pain. "Okay fine. Have it your way. We'll take care of this very soon."

Before she could respond the waiter arrived with their food. He stared at Tucker's hand still tucked in her hair pulling her head back. Maggie fought the embarrassment. He wouldn't understand that she wanted this from Tucker. He probably thought she was being harassed.

After a few tense seconds, Tucker eased his grip and slipped his hand free. An odd mixture of relief and disappointment washed over her. Her appetite for food had dimmed in the midst of Tucker's confessions. He'd told her several of his wants and the immediate urge to give him what he needed over came her.

The waiter set down their plates and asked Tucker if he required anything else. Tucker winked at him and told him no. She stared down at her exquisitely-prepared chicken and wished she still wanted to eat it.

"What's wrong, Maggie? Are you not happy with your food?"

She glanced up at him. Fuck he looked gorgeous. *Don't look at his mouth.* The second she thought it, his lips became her new obsession. Even pursed in a slight frown, he had the most kissable lips she'd ever seen. Was that weird to say about a guy? She didn't care. He had a mouth she'd give anything to have on her body again.

"Oh no, it looks delicious." She picked up her napkin and placed it on her lap before lifting her fork and digging in. If getting through dinner meant they'd get to the fun quicker, she'd eat anything he put in front of her.

"Questions," Tucker began. "I imagine we both will have them. Shall I start or do you want to go first?"

A million thoughts whirred through her mind. What did she want to know? As inquisitive as she tended to be it shocked her to draw a blank at a time like this.

When her answer wasn't forthcoming he started. "Tonight we will be in public. You'll be watching many things including others fucking. Are you ready for that?"

She worked to swallow the fork of chicken she'd just shoveled in her mouth. Every time he spoke bluntly, her pussy heated and her muscles clenched, reminding her of the toy still buried in her backside. For a second she found it hard to breathe.

"Yes," she panted.

Tucker leaned close to her ear, "I can see how aroused you are. Your nipples are so hard they are poking at the fabric of your dress. I can't wait to get you naked so I can lick them and hear you moan."

Maggie whimpered. Oh God. Her fork clattered on the plate where she'd dropped it.

His voice deepened to almost a growl, "I didn't get to fuck you last time. Now I'm dying for you."

About the time she clutched the edge of the table hoping to get her body under control, a low moan sounded from across the room. Maggie's gaze shot to the table directly across from them where the woman sat with her back pinned to the wall, her eyes closed and her mouth open panting for breath. She looked like…

"Oh my God. Is she—?"

"About to have an orgasm? I think so. Although her Dom is probably making her fight it."

She didn't understand. What kind of restaurant had he brought her to? "Tucker, what is going on?" she whispered.

He lifted her hand and brought it to his mouth. "The night I should have given you in the first place, pet. Now turn your head and watch her. You don't want to miss anything."

Confused and compelled at the same time, Maggie turned her head slowly toward the table in time to see the pretty brunette fling her head back and open her mouth to a silent moan.

"It wouldn't do for her to make a lot of noise. While the diners in the back room are on board with what goes on here, the front room is potentially a mix of lifestylers and possible vanillas that wandered in."

"Why take the risk?"

"Sometimes, part of the allure for both Dom and sub is the very real fear of someone seeing them who shouldn't."

A sudden shiver worked up Maggie's spine. He didn't need to explain further, she completely understood. The night of her arrest she'd stood outside the BDSM club wrestling with those very thoughts. Her brain kept saying what she'd been about to do was wrong on so many levels, yet she'd entered not five minutes later with the full intention of following through on her mission. After ten years of nothing but a vibrator, she would experience her heart's desire in any way her Dom for the evening chose.

"You know exactly what I mean."

He didn't phrase it as a question because he didn't need to. The damn man had seen through her in an instant. It worried her how easily he did that. Distracted by her thoughts, Maggie almost missed the Dom slipping his hand under the table. She imagined his fingers leading a trail along the woman's thighs to her most likely uncovered pussy. Would he push his fingers into her cunt or did he have a toy at the ready to drive her completely insane?

Her sex squeezed. She whimpered, her legs falling open like she imagined the other woman having done under her table. An intense ache had begun to build inside Maggie and her skin sizzled everywhere. Tucker's breath tickled the shell of her ear. Was this what it was like to be driven mad? He'd simply ordered her to watch another woman receive pleasure and she ached.

Tucker moved closer and pressed the full length of his hard body to her side. Sensations flooded through her. It was all Maggie could do to catch a breath.

"I remember what it looks like to have you tied and spread, ready to receive punishment or pleasure. It's an image I can't get out of my head.

And if it wasn't in my mind every waking moment, it's there in vivid color on a larger-than-life canvas.

She sucked in her breath. Her heart pounded. "You finished your painting? Already?"

"It's the only reason it took me so long to contact you. I couldn't do anything but paint. You consumed me," he murmured the last into her ear in a barely there hoarse whisper.

Her body jerked. The movement set off the nerves in her ass where the toy still lodged. If it was possible to come without touch, this would be the time. The woman across the room had remained silent, but her torso thrashed against the leather booth behind her. A second man had joined her and her Dom and he leaned back and watched the show.

The decadence of this place was too much. "Tucker...Sir...I want to come."

"Mmm. Four little words I love to hear." He lifted his head and cupped her chin, bringing her head around till she met his gaze. "Want to come or need to come? There's a difference."

She wanted to disagree but she couldn't form the words. When the woman across from her began to explode, her Dom covered her mouth with his hand to muffle her scream. Shocked and turned on beyond belief, Maggie stared. Moments later, the woman turned and caught Maggie's gaze.

Heat flushed her body. Embarrassment began to take over. Before she could turn her gaze away, two fingers pushed into her pussy. Fortunately, Tucker captured her strangled cry when his mouth slammed down on hers. Talk about consumed. Every nerve ending fired, sending her careening into release.

Tucker wrapped his hand around her neck and pressed them impossibly closer, while his tongue slid sensuously against hers. Maggie clung to him, her fingers digging into his forearms. Like a rock, strong and immovable he held her tight and drank down all of her cries and whimpers. Maggie had spread her legs so wide under the table, it wouldn't take much for Tucker to slide his big cock inside her. The orgasm had not abated an ounce of her need like she'd expected. If he asked her to get on her hands and knees in front of all these people so he could fuck her, there was no doubt in her mind she'd happily do it.

God, what was she thinking?

Tucker lifted his lips, "What's wrong?"

"Nothing." She pushed the word from her lips while trying to catch her breath.

"Another lie? Are you sure that's how you want to play this, Maggie? Your punishments are beginning to rack up."

"I'm sorry, I—I…" Before she could finish her thought, a small redheaded woman in an extremely short dress crawled from beneath the table across the room. Maggie gaped. The woman's lips were puffy and slick, making it obvious exactly what she'd been doing under there. The second Dom who'd joined the table removed a leash from his pocket, fastened it to the thick collar wrapped around the woman's neck and simply led her away from the table without uttering a word.

A soft chuckle from Tucker finally drew her attention away from their table. "You should see your face. I couldn't have planned something more shocking if I'd tried."

"I don't know what to say." She felt her face flame red and she cursed her fair skin. Why was it ridiculously easy to make her blush? An educated woman who studied sexuality had no business acting like a teenage schoolgirl when faced with the very activities she claimed to be an expert on.

Who was she kidding? Tucker had a way of throwing her off balance every time she went near him.

Without another word, Tucker stood from their booth, took her hand and pulled her to standing next to him. Even with the four inch fuck me heels he'd given her, he still towered over her. The top of her head reached the middle of his chest. And what a chest it was. The expensive shirt he wore looked as if it had been specifically tailored to emphasize his broad physique. The fabric clung to all the right places, making her mouth water at the vision he presented.

"What are we doing?" The question automatically fell from her mouth, while her brain zeroed in on his forearms. They were strong like concrete, but lovingly crafted by hard work with his hands. She loved touching him and it was crazy difficult to keep from doing so now.

Tucker lifted her chin. "Do you want to come with me tonight? If you aren't ready, say the word. We can go slower, but damn, Maggie, every minute I'm with you makes me want you even more. All of you, though, not just your curiosity this time, baby. I want it all."

She swallowed. It didn't take a genius to know exactly what he meant. He aimed to get inside her and see how far she wanted to go. He wanted her full submission. The million butterflies in her stomach went crazy all at once. She wanted this and this time she wouldn't run.

"I want this too, Sir."

Five simple words was all it took. The expression on his face sharpened and the look of lust he wore took on a sharper edge. He looked like a hungry beast and she felt like his next meal. Her pussy heated and her nipples hardened to tight points. The lack of a bra with this dress made her reactions obvious and she knew he didn't miss them. His lips turned up at the edges a moment before he turned on his heel with her in tow.

Instead of taking her to the front door like she'd expected, he turned toward the back of the restaurant and the hallway that housed the restrooms. Illicit images of him having his way with her here in a public place tumbled wildly through her mind. Her breath hitched and her skin tingled. A sense of urgent need swept through her. God, she'd never felt such intense longing. Fuck that. She needed to call it what it was. Tucker turned her inside out and upside down to the point she was ready to drop and fuck at a moment's notice.

In the past, it took quite a bit of build up or seduction before her body began to respond. With Tucker, a look, a word and she was embarrassingly wet and ready.

To her dismay, they passed the bathrooms and the possibility of quick satisfaction seemed unlikely. Instead he opened an unmarked door at the end of the hall with a key card he'd produced from his pocket. Thoroughly confused, Maggie passed through the door and found herself plunged into darkness.

"Tucker?" She spun back to the door and sought answers.

"Easy, sub. You're safe and sound here with me."

A small amount of light began to fill the room, which she now recognized as some sort of staff locker room. In the middle of the space sat an oversized black leather couch with tables at each end atop plush, dark carpeting. As she turned and surveyed the room, she found the walls were covered with different sized lockers and not much else. Staff room or not, the luxurious tone of the restaurant had been carried into the back rooms as well. The soft lighting from sconces on the wall added to the ambiance, further surprising her that a business would go to such trouble for their staff.

"Are we supposed to be back here?" she whispered.

"Everything is fine, little one. I know exactly what I'm doing." He closed the door to the outside and she watched him flip the lock. Before she could open her mouth to ask another question, he'd crossed the room and moved his big body into her personal space. "I've already given you more than enough opportunity to change your mind tonight. Now it's time to obey. Show me your breasts."

Maggie sucked in a breath at the unexpected request. Such a demand might have been met with resistance from any other man, but not from Tucker. He'd used that commanding tone that sent a delicious shiver down her spine. She raised her hands and reached behind her neck for the knot that held the halter of her dress together.

An odd feeling came over her. Until this week, her sex life compared to her research had been down right laughable. There'd been no adventure with her ex husband. They lived separate lives under the same roof.

So much of her life had been tied up in what she was supposed to do or what was expected of her. Tonight wasn't like that. When she'd accepted Tucker's gift and met him at this place, she'd finally shaken off the weight of her old life, giving her permission to start over.

She released the ties and allowed the halter to fall away. Cold air rushed over her skin and puckered her already sensitive nipples. Just being in the same space as Tucker had her on edge. Add to that the little BDSM touches he'd included in their evening thus far and her body had begun to simmer a long time ago.

"God, you're so beautiful." He wet one finger and circled her nipple. "These are beautiful."

The simple touch of Tucker's wet heat set her blood to sizzling. Her areola tightened with a sweet ache she wanted more of. Fortunately her mind cleared long enough for her to remember her manners. "Thank you, Sir."

He smiled and that simple act made any last reservation about standing half naked in an employee lounge disappear. With both hands now gently squeezing her breasts and plucking at her nipples, her core contracted, building the arousal another notch higher. Much more of this and he could do anything he wanted. She sighed and closed her eyes.

"No, Maggie. Keep your eyes open and on me." That voice slid through her consciousness like a sharp blade, alerting her to his displeasure. Her eyes snapped open.

"Much better." He slid his hand in her hair and yanked her into his arms. There was no chance to breathe before he captured her mouth and fiercely kissed her. He wasted no time pushing apart her lips and thrusting his tongue inside. She groaned. The sheer force of his intensity made her weak in the knees. Good thing he held her to him, since he made it impossible for a girl to maintain her balance on four-inch heels.

She grabbed his biceps. The hard planes of muscle flexed and bunched under her fingertips. How had she ever imagined him as easy going—or dare she say boring? He was intense and rough, exactly as she'd always desired. A sudden pinch to her right nipple caught her off guard. As pain exploded, she gasped into his mouth. His animalistic and potentially out of control behavior pushed every damn button she possessed. Another light caress, even more dangerous than a pinch, because the pain gave way to more sizzling pleasure.

As suddenly as he'd grabbed her, he released her. Maggie wobbled on her heels until he steadied her with a grip on her elbow. Her body had gone soft and mushy.

"I could take you here and now. You'd say yes and beg me for more."

Her sex squeezed at his sensual threat. She wanted it. Just as he'd said, the danger of being caught only made it all the more thrilling. He'd tapped into another of her weaknesses whether he realized it or not. She imagined him pushing her to her hands and knees and subjecting her to a hard ride. This time her arousal coated her sex. Her body was even more eager than her mind. The last few days of heightened emotions and confusion came to a head in that moment. She needed him.

"Turn around and hold your hands clasped together at the small of your back," he commanded.

Unsure of his latest request she stammered, "Yes—Yes, Sir." Pushing aside the small shred of doubt that had popped up, Maggie turned and placed her hands as he'd asked. Facing away from him, a little of her previous confidence faltered. She missed his touch on her breasts. A glance down showed the evidence of what he'd done. Her nipples stood erect and aching.

His hands skimmed down her side and settled into the curve of her waist for a moment before continuing to the hem of her dress. He pulled the fabric out of his way and grasped the naked globes of her ass, spreading her cheeks. "If you haven't already figured it out, I'm a serious ass man. And I have big plans for this one." He squeezed her flesh tight and then took a step back. "Bend down, legs straight, head toward your knees."

With her heart hammering against her chest, Maggie carefully leaned forward as far as she could while still maintaining balance. It didn't take a genius to realize Tucker now had a fully open view to her plugged asshole and her freshly-shaved pussy. Both of which only made her hotter. God, she really did want him to fuck her now. She ached for it.

With her thoughts running wild and wanton about Tucker pulling his cock out and shoving it into her, she started to lose it when he began tapping on the toy sitting snug inside her. "I'm going to fuck this gorgeous ass later," he promised. His finger circled the wide base of the plug and Maggie swore black spots swam in her vision. Nerves flared to life and she couldn't have withheld the low moan if she'd tried.

Instead of him moving closer like she wanted, she felt him step away. A soft cry escaped her lips.

"I know, baby. But not yet. I promised you a night in Purgatory and that's what you're going to get."

Metal clanged behind her and she realized he'd accessed one of the lockers that ran the full length of the wall behind her. Moments later, he pressed against her backside and squeezed her clasped hands. Something unknown and strange rubbed against the skin of her right hand. "Feel this?" he asked.

"Yes, Sir," she answered. Her stomach trembled and her sex squeezed. He'd found rope.

"Before we head into the club, I'm going to bind you. You'll have full vision for everything going on but you won't be able to touch anything or stop anyone from touching you."

"What?" she blurted.

His finger tightened on a nipple in clear

disapproval. "There's a private party going on tonight, so the rules are different than usual. Any Dom is allowed to touch an uncollared sub and her bare flesh without asking for permission." He reached around her and flicked one of her nipples. "So in your case, they'll have free rein to touch these."

She shivered at the thought of a variety of men being allowed to touch her at their will and her accepting it with no questions asked. This wasn't a simple fantasy anymore. Her body was about to be put on display in a public club where everything she'd researched had the potential of becoming a reality. Every muscle in her lower body squeezed at the image. Her pussy ached. This wasn't the time to analyze everything that happened around her. It was her chance to let Tucker take control and allow her to feel. No matter what happened, she believed he would protect her from anything she couldn't handle.

He slid his hand around to her backside again and this time her skirt shifted and his fingers prodded her cleft, sliding easily through the moisture gathered there.

"That's what I thought. You're so wet."

A flood of heat filled her face. He was right of course. She wanted more. Whatever he needed, she needed.

"You still have a safeword and I expect you to use it if you need to, Maggie. I want to push you but don't be afraid to stop when things go too far." He nuzzled her ear with his lips. "I know how you subs are. Always ready to please, sometimes to your own detriment. The club also accepts the word red as a universal safeword in case I am not within hearing distance." With one finger he pinched her clit, bringing her into sharper focus. "I'm not kidding here, Maggie. If I catch you too afraid to stop a scene you don't like, I will punish you until you can't sit the next day."

Her head swam with all this new information. Every time a new fear cropped into her head, Tucker responded like he'd read her mind.

"I don't understand."

"Body language, little one. It gives you away every time. From the wet cunt to the frightened look in your eyes. I'll know. Now be still so I can get these knots tied."

With the first slide of the rope underneath her left arm she sighed. For years she'd admired many erotic photographs of women tied in various bondage and become aroused. The first tie landed in the middle of her upper back, leaving a straight band of rope across her chest above her breasts. With the second an exact duplicate of the first except below her boobs. His movements were quick and deft.

"You've done this before." She didn't realize she'd spoken out loud until he chuckled behind her.

"Yes, little one. I am far from innocent."

"So this is something you do with every sub you play with?" She couldn't help herself. For a minute, doubt began creeping back in. The thought of her being just another woman in the long line of women he kept didn't sit right.

He grabbed the tied rope and pulled her back sharply. "Don't do that," he warned. "What I did in the past has nothing to do with the present. I'm here with you because I need you. This is nothing like the past."

The tone of disgust in his voice when he spoke the word past left Maggie with questions. What in the hell had happened to him? She longed to be facing him now, looking into his eyes and searching for the answers she *needed*. The urge to comfort him overwhelmed her.

"I'm sorry, Sir." It was all she could offer him while he continued to tie her. One section at a time. No more words passed between them as he worked. He briefly stepped to her side to bring the rope over her shoulders so he could tie them at the front between her breasts, creating a halter. Maggie gasped when his knuckles brushed her sensitive skin. Since when did her chest become so ridiculously erogenous? She tried to meet his gaze, but his focus was now on the rope.

The next tie bound the bottom and top bands around her breasts with one knot in the front. He moved behind her and tightened the rope. Maggie glanced down to see her boobs bulging between the royal blue strands. She grit her teeth. As if she wasn't already aching enough.

Finally, he arranged her hands so each one was gripping the opposite forearm behind her back, creating a perfect square with her arms. He then fastened the rope around her wrist several times, checking each wrap with a finger to prevent cutting off her circulation. Of course with the secure position of her arms, her breasts were thrust forward. She'd never seen them look this inviting before. Her stomach fluttered. There was going to be a lot of touching tonight. Her gut felt it.

Tucker's heat disappeared from her backside as she imagined him studying his work. "Beautiful. Now you're ready."

"But I don't— We aren't at the club. I can't go back into the restaurant like this."

He chuckled, the sound so close to her ear, her body clenched again. She might question him but in reality, her resistance had dissolved the minute he'd called her for another chance. She craved this more than anything else. "You're right, you can't. You need a little more warming up."

He grabbed her hair and turned her in the direction of the couch in the middle of the room. With his knee behind her leg, he pushed her face down onto the cushion with her knees underneath her and her ass high in the air.

"Time to check on this asshole. I hope you lubed it well like you were instructed." With one hand he spread her cheeks and the other he tapped lightly against the plastic, creating sharp vibrations that lit her nerves on fire.

"Ohhh…" she moaned, unable to control her response.

"If my driver had brought you around from the other side of the building you'd have probably noticed the small Purgatory sign. This restaurant is attached on the back side and shares its owners with the fetish club. For certain club members, for whom discretion is key, this room provides a private entrance."

The way he kept touching her made it really difficult for her to concentrate on what he said. Something about a private entrance and the restaurant. Maggie shifted, lifting her bottom for more of Tucker's touch. Her move was met with a resounding smack on her bare ass that sent fire streaking along her thighs and down to her pussy. Was everything connected to her sex?

"Be still and take what I give you, little one." He began pulling on the plug embedded in her tight entrance and all thought of words fled. Her body tightened.

"No, Maggie. Relax. The less you fight the easier it will be."

She worked to follow his instruction by focusing on relaxing her muscle groups one by one until she'd practically melted into the soft cushion beneath her.

This time he pulled on the flared edge and it slid easily from her aching anus while dragging across nerve endings she hadn't expected. She'd tried this once on her own and she'd experienced nothing but frustrations over how uncomfortable she'd been. That same edge of discomfort still existed but the excitement Tucker's domination created easily overtook the pain to give her pleasure. Something in her core shifted as she opened more to his demands.

His body shifted and — *Holy Shit* — somewhere in all this he'd freed his cock. The white-hot poker of his rigid erection pressed against her backside.

CHAPTER TEN

Tucker watched Maggie's eyes widen at the sight of his erection. Yes, her obvious pleasure fed his ego like nobody's business, but who was he kidding? He was so ramped up on this woman all his brain focused on was how to get inside her now. Their night a few days ago had left him with an ache and it had since evolved into full-blown obsession.

He fed the butt plug back into her eager little hole with ease. Her tension levels were changing and soon she'd be ready for him to take her there. Once the toy was again seated fully inside her, he grabbed her hips and lifted her knees from the furniture. With her back arched, he zeroed in on the sight of her gorgeous cunt. Slick with her desire, he found her impossible to resist on any level. Especially this one. He leaned forward and slid his tongue between the plump folds of her pussy. The resulting cry from his new sub's mouth made him smile.

"Oh yes. Oh please, Sir."

The barely whispered plea hammered at his conscience. Tonight he wanted Maggie to get everything she'd been dreaming of when it came to her research. He hoped that a night in Purgatory would be the perfect remedy to erase her prior experience from her mind. If those bullshit charges against her hadn't been dropped, he'd have likely unleashed hell on earth, AKA his lawyer.

He forcibly pushed outside thoughts from his mind and zeroed in on the goal in front of him. He was still a selfish man. One with every intention of worshipping Maggie with his tongue and cock until she pleaded for mercy. Tucker lapped at her flesh again, this time making certain to cross over her more sensitive areas. He wouldn't be satisfied until he'd claimed every inch of her luscious body and mind.

As near to losing control as he could afford, Tucker placed her knees back on the couch, parted her pussy lips with one hand and nudged her opening with the head of his cock.

Maggie turned her head to look at him.

"Eyes front. Stay in position."

"Yes, Sir," she responded while moving back into place. "I only wanted to see your face when I asked you to please fuck me."

Tucker ground his teeth and tried to hold back from her. It wouldn't do to let her know how easily she could manipulate him. His hands tightened around her hips. Seconds ticked by. Like it or not he was losing the battle.

"Please," she whispered, the guttural tone going

straight to his dick, snapping the last of his control.

He shoved forward, driving his cock through tight muscle and warm heat. His vision wavered. Maggie gasped. For a few moments he couldn't move. The base of his spine tingled, letting him know that if he wasn't careful it'd be all over before they got started. Which was exactly what he got for denying himself the last time they were together.

No control.

Fine tremors erupted under his hands as Maggie, too, struggled with the overload of sensations. He smiled. He'd forgotten how much he liked watching a sub struggle to be good and follow his instructions with his cock buried inside her. With her, it seemed even better. The idea of his Maggie precariously perched on the edge drove him a little crazy.

"You're mine now, baby. I hope you understand that." Not looking for an answer, Tucker pulled from her clasp and immediately drove forward again harder than before. She squeaked her surprise. Pleased, he did it again and again, setting a harsh driving rhythm that left no question about his intentions.

He'd not forbidden her to speak or make noise because he didn't care who heard them or came to investigate. The staff here were hand-chosen from the BDSM community and well-versed in what to expect from many of their patrons. If they passed by the door and heard Maggie's moans, they wouldn't blink an eye.

With every clutching pass, Maggie pulled Tucker deeper. He dug his fingers into her buttocks and rode her every bit as rough as he'd dreamt these last several days. He needed to come. It was that thought that finally brought Tucker racing back to reality. He jerked back and stumbled a couple of feet before catching his balance.

"No…" she protested.

Tucker ignored her pleas. Holy fucking shit motherfucker. He'd forgotten a condom. Not once in his sexual life had he forgotten to wear protection. He closed his eyes and prayed for sanity. Obviously three days of seclusion with nothing to think about other than Maggie's perfect submission had made him crazy. He looked down at the succulent flesh of her pussy and sighed. It wasn't too late.

Doubt crowded his mind. His vow from years ago to leave this lifestyle behind floated at the edges of his conscience. Tucker tightened down the memories and ground down on his jaw. This was different. Maggie was different.

As much as he hated to do it, he shoved his stiff-as-a board cock back into his pants. For now, they'd both learn the hard lesson of denial. He flipped Maggie's skirt down and gently helped her to her feet. He could see it was a struggle for her in the shoes he'd purchased but damn if her legs didn't look incredible. Unfortunately, a small frown marred her beautiful face.

"Don't fret. It'll be better this way. There will be a lot of things you'll see tonight that turn you on and keep you on the edge. It might not seem like it now, but trust me it's a very good place to be." To reinforce his statement, he pulled her into his arms and placed soft kisses along the seam of her mouth and jaw line.

"I'm beginning to worry you might be more evil than I originally believed."

He grinned down at her. "It's the pretty face. Fools them every time." He cupped her chin and lifted her head sharply even though she'd already been looking at him. "You're smarter than most girls though, aren't you Miss Maggie. So smart, you think you know all there is to know because you've spent a decade researching."

"I know a lot. It should be enough to keep me out of trouble." He watched her body stiffen, her eyes grow wary.

"If that were true, I don't think you'd have run from my house like a scared jack rabbit."

"I don't think—"

"Enough." He covered her mouth with his hand and tightened his arm around her shoulders. "I don't require anymore explanations at this point. What I do need is a sub who listens. One who obeys." He gentled his hand across her face. "Purgatory generally doesn't have a lot of strict protocol in the club area. A lot of first timers come in and say and do things that cause some of the regulars to roll their eyes. But we aren't going to the main floor. I prefer to keep this first visit a bit more intimate."

She nodded, the relief obvious in her expression.

"The members only section of the club has certain expectations for all their Dominants and subs. Especially the uncollared subs like you." Tucker released her mouth and waited for the rapid-fire questions that never came. "If you appear less than one hundred percent into what we're doing, you'll end up fair game for the other Doms."

"Seriously?" she blurted.

"Yes, seriously. Not all who come here are in it for the strict rules and protocols, but they've been set up nonetheless to keep the peace. As long as we're together, if anyone wants to play with you, they'll ask me first. It will be *my* choice to say yes or no."

Her eyes grew wide at his implication. Of course her nipples also grew tighter and he imagined her pussy wetter. Damn, he loved her easy responses and lack of desire to hide them. Tucker skimmed his hand down her side and gripped her hip, pulling her tight against his body. He didn't want her to forget for an instant what she did to him.

"You're not ready for that, little one." He nipped at her ear lobe. "I haven't had nearly enough of you yet to even consider sharing anything beyond a few touches." If he hadn't been so in tuned to her body's reactions, he might have missed the tiny shudder that trembled through her.

"We could always skip the club and go home instead."

He drew back and stared down into her face. "Don't think I haven't considered it. But I have specific goals for tonight and I'm nothing if not goal-oriented."

In an unexpected sweet gesture, Maggie laid her head on his shoulder and sighed into him. "Whatever you wish, Sir."

His groin tightened again. Dear God, how much of this could he take before he exploded? For a fleeting second, he considered scooping her into his arms and rushing them back to his place. He had no doubt all the D/s she needed could be found in private.

"You've grown quite compliant, little sub. You'll quickly learn your sweet submission drives me wild," he sighed and peeled her from his chest, "but a deal is a deal and we're going in. Ready?"

She lowered her eyes and nodded her head. Tucker took a deep breath. It was going to take some digging deep to keep his restraint in place. He grasped her hand and tugged her under his left arm. Now, if only his gut would stop twisting. He'd control his nerves at any cost.

CHAPTER ELEVEN

Maggie squeezed her eyes shut and sent out a small prayer that nothing bad would happen this time. It was damned hard not to think about her last experience as Tucker walked her through an adjoining door that led them into the Purgatory club.

To her surprise, when they crossed the threshold they walked into another empty hallway, not the extravagant club she'd expected. She turned and met Tucker's gaze. "I don't understand."

"Private entrance, remember? If we were going through the front door you'd have been required to wear a little more clothing."

Great. Him mentioning her state of undress reminded her what she'd agreed to. She faltered on the treacherous heels.

Tucker grabbed her arm and steadied her. "Easy little one. You don't have anything to be afraid of." He tweaked a nipple between his fingers. "Of course, the nerves are a different story. I'd be more concerned if you weren't nervous."

"I know," she replied, "I just need this to be okay, if you know what I mean."

"I do." He reached for another door and twisted the knob. "And now it's time to make some new memories to overshadow the old."

The moment the door cracked, a cacophony of sound streamed from the opposite side. People talking, hard-edged scene music she'd learned to love through her research, and the unmistakable sound of a whip cracking against waiting flesh.

Her sex squeezed. She'd taken a group whip class from a master teacher at a convention once. There wasn't much chance she'd ever wield one like a pro but the instructor had left an impression. Since then the distinct sound of a whip whistling through the air revved her up.

Tucker ushered her inside and closed the door behind them. Maggie waited several seconds for her vision to adjust to the low-level ambient lighting that glowed from a series of sconces on the walls and then her eyes went wide with the sights in front of her. They'd entered a room the size of a grand ballroom in a high-end hotel and every ounce as elegant. From rich velvet wall coverings to the allure of glittering chandeliers, the room whispered money in a not so subtle way. But this wasn't like any ballroom she'd been in before. From end to end there was play equipment set up from the simple spanking benches she'd seen before to some equipment she didn't recognize at all. Even more interesting was the variety of people that filled the room.

Every size, shape and generation engaged in play as well as many onlookers who appeared to be enjoying the view. The music drowned out any voices, instead focusing the participants and onlookers on the scenes playing out in front of them.

The sounds of a buzzing crackle caught Maggie's attention as her gaze sought the source. She didn't have to wait long. A large crowd had formed around one of the alcoves not far from where she stood. From there she made out the familiar glow of the violet wand. Familiar only to her through research and online videos. She'd always been curious...

Mesmerized she took a small step in that direction. A firm tug on her rope harness stopped her from wandering away. "It's always one of the most popular play stations in the house," Tucker whispered at her ear. "One I'd happily introduce you to when you're ready."

Maggie's breath hitched. The sound of his voice snapped her back to reality. Yes, she'd come to observe and learn what happens in a private BDSM club, but more importantly she'd come here to be with Tucker. Everything else was secondary.

"I want you to explore, but you need to keep your head and try not to wander away from me."

"Yes, Sir," she answered easily. Little did he know, every time she called him Sir, her stomach jolted, making blood rush to certain parts. Maggie paused. Maybe he did know. Experienced Doms were said to be very aware of their sub's desires and their reactions.

She swung around and faced Tucker. "Is that what it's like for you?"

His forehead wrinkled as he looked down at her. "What on earth are you talking about?"

She laughed. It was easy to forget that she tended to have full conversations with herself in her head that no one else heard. "Sorry. I was just wondering if it's easy for you to read a submissive's needs through their body language."

Tucker drew her into his arms, crushing her breasts against the soft material of his shirt. For a second the sensations swam through her head, making her forget she'd even asked a question. Her nipples were more sensitive than ever and the slightest touch to the aroused skin threatened to set her off. Of course there was also his delicious scent that made her want to bury her face in his chest.

"Doms aren't mind readers, Maggie. Although I have studied body language in all its forms extensively. A lifetime ago I thought I was pretty good at it and it has often served me well."

For a brief moment she noticed an odd, far away look in his eyes before he refocused on her and the heat of desire bored into her instead. Had that been sadness?

"Are you sure you want to be here?" The

question popped out of her mouth before she could stop it.

His gaze darkened. In the span of a heartbeat, she had no idea what he'd do next. His hand moved to her chin and tilted her head farther than necessary for her to meet his eyes. "You, little one, are headed for trouble. Relax, follow and observe. And above all else trust me if you can. Trust me to give you what you need tonight."

It was strange how comfortable she felt with him. She nodded her head and he frowned. Oops. She'd forgotten again the direct answer he preferred. "Yes, Sir."

He smiled, but it didn't quite seem real. "Very good," he offered before unpeeling her from his chest. The rush of cool air puckered her nipples. Maggie's sharp intake of breath set off a chuckle from Tucker.

"Your responsiveness is incredible."

Maggie lowered her lashes and grappled with composure when at the moment she wasn't above getting down on her knees and begging him to take her. There was so much she wanted to see but only one thing she wanted to do. Suddenly, all the trappings of a public club no longer appealed. If Tucker wanted to be her Dom, they didn't need any of this to make it happen.

"What's wrong?"

"Nothing—I mean—I don't know," she stammered, "I was so excited by the thought of finally seeing a public dungeon. Now I don't remember why it was so important."

"You're here tonight because it's what I want. I desire to show you some of what you missed out on before and to learn more about what turns you off and on."

"But I—"

"Enough with the reasoning," he snapped. "You're my sub and if I want you here then that is enough. There isn't always going to be a grand scheme and you won't get to plan every detail when it comes to our relationship. I'll make the rules based on what I've learned and you'll choose to either follow them or not."

Maggie's insides quivered under the change in tone. He'd cranked the Dom voice to high and it was enough to make her knees knock together. She loved it.

"Your response is…"

"Yes, Sir. Thank you, Sir." She couldn't get the words out fast enough.

"Good. Now turn around and let the crowd see you. They're waiting."

"What?" Her stomach dropped to her feet.

"Maggie," he spoke sharply. That was all it took to make her realize they had an audience and if she pushed much farther things might get out of hand like he'd mentioned before. She slowly twirled on her too-high heels and came face to face with numerous faces watching their exchange with different levels of interest. A few of the submissives dared small smiles while many of the Doms looked on disapprovingly. Before either of them made a move, three people broke from the crowd and headed their way. A lovely submissive wearing nothing but an underbust corset and a thick collar around her neck and two male Doms each holding a chain that attached to small D-rings on the woman's leather collar.

Maggie tried not to stare at the other woman's nudity but it was impossible not to. The men beside her were gorgeous but she stood out anyway. The woman had the body of Venus and Maggie wasn't sure she'd ever seen such gorgeous curves in her life.

The pretty submissive caught her gaze and smiled knowingly. Maggie felt the rush of heat equal to a thousand suns fill her cheeks. Caught red-handed, she didn't know how to react. The thought of turning to Tucker and burying her head in his chest again certainly appealed. But she'd done enough already to embarrass him without making things worse.

"Tucker!" one man called out. "Leo mentioned he'd seen you the other night and I didn't believe him." He held out his hand and Tucker took it in his for a quick shake.

"You should know better than to doubt Leo. He's not the one who's so fond of gossip." A wicked smile crossed Tucker's face.

The bald man on the other side of the submissive laughed. "Poor Quinn, he forgets how long a memory you have."

"Tucker knows I'm only giving him a hard time."

Maggie sensed an awkwardness she didn't understand. Fortunately, Leo stepped forward and spoke.

"Have you brought us a present tonight?" Leo asked. The other man's gaze raked over her body, a smile crossing his face.

It was all Maggie could do not to squirm.

Tucker's arm wrapped tight around her waist and pulled her against his side. "Fraid not. This one's all mine."

"Spoil sport." Tucker and Quinn laughed while Leo gave her one last lingering once over. "She looks like fun."

Maggie lowered her eyes. She had the feeling the more she gawked at the men the more encouraged they'd become.

"Well, you're just in time for Katie's final punishment. It's been one hell of a week."

The gorgeous woman next to him perked up. She glanced at Leo first and then turned to Quinn who bent to whisper something in her ear. The resulting smile made some of the knots in Maggie's stomach loosen. It was obvious these two men held a great amount of affection for their submissive. She hoped Tucker wanted to watch.

"Sounds perfect. This is my sub's first visit to Purgatory."

A tall, broad shouldered man appeared before them, the Purgatory emblem across his chest her first clue he was some sort of employee.

"It's time, Sirs. The stage is set."

All of them turned in the direction the man pointed. A raised stage was perfectly placed in the middle of the ballroom.

Leo glanced at Tucker. "It's good seeing you back at the club, Tuck. I hope this means we'll be seeing more of you."

Tucker only raised his chin before the two men moved off taking their submissive with them. Maggie watched them disappear into the crowd as they weaved their way to center stage.

"Come, little one. I think you'll want to see this."

He found them a spot a few rows back, where he took a seat before pulling Maggie into his lap. She squeaked as she landed on his thighs with an embarrassingly ungraceful plop. "Sorry."

"Considering you're right where I wanted, there is nothing to be sorry for." He kept his voice low and rich, the timbre working its way through her tight muscles. "Kiss me."

She automatically responded to the command. With a slight bend of her neck, she pressed her lips to his, opening on a sigh when she felt his tongue working into her mouth. The simple kiss grew hotter and Maggie squirmed in his lap.

All too soon, he broke the kiss and wrapped his hand around her shoulder. "Now turn around and be a good girl. We have a show to get through before I can have my way with you."

Forced to face front, Maggie worked to keep from frowning. Didn't he understand yet that she'd come for him. Everything else seemed unimportant anymore.

Then the rest of the dim lights in the club winked out and the hum of the excited crowd grew louder. She gasped when a spotlight came on and illuminated a large piece of equipment standing on the stage with Katie already in place only a few feet away. Maggie clamped her mouth shut to keep any more noises from coming out.

Oh. My. God. Was that an old-fashioned dungeon stock?

Her body went rigid at the sight. The submissive was bent at the waist and sure enough her head and arms had been placed inside wooden stocks and securely locked with big silver chains that looked impossible to escape from.

"Easy." Tucker's fingers stroked her bare hip. She hadn't even noticed him lift her dress. "It's only a scene and one that was well-negotiated I can assure you."

"How?" Maggie whispered. "How can you *really* know this is what she wants?" The pit in her stomach had grown from a hard knot to a fist-sized rock of dread. Seeing Katie imprisoned was eerily reminiscent of the night Maggie had been hauled to jail in handcuffs.

Before Tucker could answer, the Dom called Leo appeared at the head of the stage dressed in simple black clothing and a wicked-looking whip in his hand. Katie struggled in her cage and the air sucked from Maggie's lungs at the sound of the heavy chains clanking together.

The scene before her began to fall away and instead she saw and heard the chaos of the one club she'd dared enter before. People were screaming and yelling into the darkness, men with guns were surrounding the people. Someone grabbed Maggie from behind and pulled her arms behind her back, wrenching her shoulder. In the blink of an eye, metal scraped against her flesh moments before the locks clicked into place. Sweat trickled down her back and smoke burned her nostrils and throat.

"Maggie!" Tucker's sharp voice brought her back to the present. His arms were banded around her chest in a grip so tight she immediately knew he'd had to subdue her.

Oh God no.

To make matters worse a few of the other club goers in front of them had turned to stare.

"Are you are okay? What's wrong?"

Tears filled her eyes before she could stop them. A glance at the stage showed Leo behind Katie with his whip spinning in the air. He was about to throw a strike any second and she couldn't stand to watch it.

"Red," she croaked out, barely a whisper.

"What?" Tucker leaned forward.

"Red. Please. Red." The first tear splashed on her cheek before she uttered the last word.

To her relief, Tucker was true to his word and immediately stood, shifting her in his arms.

"We're leaving," he announced. Probably as much for the benefit of the people surrounding them as hers.

His long legs covered the space of the ballroom at lightning speed and before she had a moment to contemplate her humiliating predicament, they were in the hallway and headed back to the door that led into the restaurant.

When they entered the private lounge space, Maggie heaved a sigh of relief to find the room as empty as they'd left it. Tucker eased onto the soft leather couch and what they'd done before they went into the club flashed through her memory. The moment Tucker slid into her had been more thrilling than anything before and exactly what she'd needed. The club... It had sounded reasonable.

Without words Tucker began untying the rope binding her arms behind her back. As the bonds released, so did her breath. A strong tingling sensation ran up and down her back and into her shoulders, until Tucker began massaging her arms and neck. Then she simply wanted to melt into him.

"Look at me, Maggie."

With some reluctance, she unscrewed her eyelids and slowly cracked them open. To her surprise, there was no anger or disappointment on Tucker's face. Only small lines around his mouth and eyes where he'd furrowed his brow in concern.

"I made a mistake. You weren't ready and I assumed you were. I'm sorry."

A lump formed in her throat at the heartfelt words. It was so easy to get wrapped up into the power exchange aspect of D/s and forget that they were both still ordinary people. Well, she was ordinary. A billionaire recluse, not so much.

She struggled in his arms until he released her and she rose to her feet. The minute she landed on those crazy heels she began to wobble. She reached down and pulled one off and then the other. "It's going to take some time to get used to these."

"Hurry up, 'cause I look forward to the view of you naked in those shoes when your legs are propped on my shoulder as I slide into you."

Maggie jerked, losing her balance for a second at his words. Heat infused her face and her pussy and nipples ached at the mere imagery of his thought. "Oh, you're evil." She smiled up at him.

"Forgiven?"

He was so forgiven. She leaned forward and pressed her lips to his forehead. "Nothing to forgive. I could have said no and I didn't." She leaned back. "I waited a really long time for this. The opportunity to go in a club and observe and participate seemed like the ultimate dream. Yet, here I am scared witless and not as interested as I thought."

"Not interested in BDSM?" The skeptical look stamped across his face nearly became her undoing.

A smile tugged at the corners of her mouth. Maggie looked down at her toes and tried to still her thoughts. Tucker the Dom wouldn't appreciate her laughing in his face right now. "No, Sir. That's not what I mean at all." She took a slow, deep breath. "I always believed my research had come to a standstill because of a lack of firsthand experience, so I focused on getting into a club to fix that. Of course, everyone in the free world knows how that turned out." The urge to sink down on her knees and cuddle her head in Tucker's lap surged through her. Rather than fight the need, Maggie drifted down to the floor and took the position she couldn't fight.

Tucker immediately threaded his fingers in her hair and tugged on the short ends. "Continue," he commanded with just enough of that edge to his voice to remind her the Dom was still very close to the surface.

"It's not the club I need, it's the Dom. I think I've learned that now." Her voice had lowered to a husky whisper. Alone again with Tucker, the rash of fear she'd experienced in the club dissipated. With his hands touching her while her head rested in his lap, a sense of serenity overtook her. "I only want you, Sir."

CHAPTER TWELVE

Immense pride swept through Tucker as the sweet submissive side of Maggie took over her beautiful mind. What he'd thought had been a disastrous turn of events actually had become a turning point for her. Although the damage he'd caused by taking her to the club still weighed his mind with regret, he saw an opportunity to salvage their night. Now he only had to seize the moment and make her his.

"We're going home." And he was going to have his submissive all to himself. The way he'd truly wanted her in the first place. Tucker withdrew his phone from his pocket and texted his driver. He slid his hands under her shoulders and lifted her to his lap. He was confident she could walk out on her own but his need to hold her close for a few more minutes negated that.

Without wasting any more time, they slipped from the lounge and turned toward the rear door that led to the adjacent parking lot. Walking her out through the crowded restaurant was out of the question. Maggie had found her way to a comfortable spot with her submission and he wasn't about to break that by carrying her through a busy room. He pushed open the door and true to form, his driver stood next to the car waiting for him.

"Take us home."

"Yes, Sir." The door was opened and Tucker ducked them both into the backseat.

"That must be nice."

"What's that?"

"Having a car and driver on standby ready to whisk you away at a moment's notice."

Tucker smiled. "A successful conglomerate does have its perks."

Maggie nestled closer and Tucker gave them a few minutes for her to relax and for him to gather her thoughts. It wasn't easy with a warm, willing woman plastered to his body. He'd been hard long before she'd arrived at the restaurant and things had only progressed from there. Her still-bare breasts beckoned to him and it wasn't long before he began tracing small circles around the edges of her nipples. She was so soft and warm. He wanted to play with her all night.

"You have beautiful breasts, little one." He was immediately rewarded with puckered skin and taut nipples. Like him, her arousal had returned in full force. It didn't take long before she squirmed in his lap like a wiggly puppy.

"You're torturing me again, Tucker."

"I know." Instead of stopping, he pinched her nipples and bent forward to draw one into his mouth. This close to her skin, the soft scent of vanilla assaulted his senses. Great. She smelled like a sugar cookie and tasted like sin. The ache in his cock intensified and he wondered if it could get any worse.

It could.

She twisted and turned until the crease of her soft ass rested across his rigid erection, reminding him that she still wore his plug. A low groan escaped him. At this rate he'd be insane before they reached his house.

Fuck it. Who needed a bed?

"Roll over and present your ass, little one."

His lovely angel twisted a bit awkwardly before resettling once again with her ass in the air and her breasts squashed against the side of his legs.

"You've had a lot of leeway these last several days but you should know that as we continue I will establish rules and consequences for breaking them. There is a lot to be said for spontaneity in life but I rather enjoy making plans and seeing them through."

"I'm so—" she started to apologize again

"No. Don't. You did exactly the right thing tonight. Not every plan is perfect and it gives me a great deal of confidence that you understand the use of a safeword." He lifted her skirt and began caressing her pale cheeks. "Now I have a decision to make. Do I continue? Or do I give you a break for tonight?"

Her body jerked and she whimpered.

"That's what I thought, but first things first." He spread her ass checks and Maggie gasped. "I think you've worn this long enough. I want you ready, not sore."

"No. please. Not yet."

Tucker arched his brow. That was not the reaction he expected. "Then tell me what you want." He slid his hand along the bottom curve of her ass to the pussy below. There he ran his fingers over her slit, reveling in the moisture that taunted him. She was as ready as he was, maybe more so.

When she didn't answer, he repeated the question. "What do you want, Maggie? I want to hear it." As he moved toward her opening, she titled her hips in an obvious effort to get him to touch her at a more needed angle. Instead he withdrew his hand and swatted her ass.

"I want you inside me. Don't want to wait."

Better. She'd given him part of the truth. "Hmm. I believe you do want to be fucked but that's not all of it. What about this?" He tapped on the base of the plug until she quivered against him. Her muscles clenched and unclenched around the toy, the sight making his cock pulse in demand. If he didn't get inside her soon, his head was going to blow. "You have to be honest. If we don't learn to communicate better we'll end up making another mistake."

She turned her head and met his gaze. For a second he couldn't figure out what she was thinking. In the next moment, she struggled against his hold. "Please let me up."

He sensed a thread of steel behind her request. Curious about what the hell was going through her mind he held up his hands in mock surrender and let her push to her feet. His confusion grew as she crawled back on his lap this time straddling his legs so she faced him. As her pussy pressed against him, a renewed surge of lust grabbed him by the balls. He'd give her a moment but that's it. He didn't possess an infinite amount of patience and the memory of sinking into her heat earlier in the evening made rivulets of sweat roll down his spine as he held back.

He didn't know what to expect from her, but her cupping his face with her hands and drawing their heads close together wasn't it.

"Thank you for taking me to Purgatory. The fact you wanted to give me the experience I'd missed out on before I—"

She didn't finish the sentence, but she didn't have to. Before she was arrested hung in the air between them.

"Let's just say no one has ever done something like that before."

The sadness in her voice broke his resolve. He closed his lips over hers, stealing the kiss he needed more than breath. He roamed his hands over her hips, lifting the fabric of her dress until he found skin. A groan filled his head. As good as she'd looked in the gorgeous dress it couldn't compete with her nudity.

His choice would be to keep her hidden and naked all the time. Naked so he could touch, love or paint her any time he wanted and hidden so the cruel outside world could never touch her. There was always someone out there waiting for the right time to do something very bad. Tucker shook that idiotic though from his mind. Just because he was jaded didn't mean she had to be.

"Will you fuck me now?" Her kiss-swollen lips mesmerized him. So pink and puffy. Which of course reminded him of her pussy.

"Only if you tell me why."

Her shoulders sagged and the look of fear flashed again through her eyes before she looked away from him.

"Don't do that. Look at me and be honest. I'm not going to be upset by anything you want, darlin'." He cupped her chin and turned her to face him. "Say it."

"You are a mean man, Tucker Lewis. I want to know what it feels like to have both. Okay?"

"One dick in your ass and one in your pussy?"

The look of horror in her eyes made him smile. It baffled him how easily words embarrassed someone whose livelihood depended on both written and verbal communication.

"Fine. Yes. Are you happy now?"

Tucker arched his brow. He loved feisty, but she had a way of pushing him that went too far. Tucker grabbed her hair and slowly pulled her head back until she arched back as much as nature allowed. The slim line of her pale neck made him lean forward and nip at the tender skin followed by a slow lick toward her right ear. Her resulting shiver made him smile inside.

He firmly pinched one of her nipples, waiting for her gasp. Her arms jerked, coming up to grab his arms and the hand in her hair tightened, assuring he had her fully restrained. "No more games, Maggie. You'll do only what I want. What I give you permission to. Because that's what you want isn't it?"

*

Maggie swallowed hard against the jolt of sensation across her clit. Part of her wanted to say no, but they'd both know that was a lie. She wanted this man with a passion she hadn't felt in so very very long. The idea of him taking what he wanted made her insides quiver and her pussy crazy wet. The feeling of her body being stretched to his will thrilled her. It was so damned freeing.

The pressure at her nipples intensified until holding in her reaction was no longer possible.

"Tucker," she whined.

"Really? That's what you're going to call me now?"

"No, Sir," she breathed through the flare of pain he inflicted moments before he released her and bent to take the aching flesh in his mouth.

Oh shit.

The lash of his tongue felt like heaven. Soft, wet and wonderfully warm. She sighed. Between the fiery fire and the building hunger she stood on the precipice of insanity.

"You're driving me crazy, angel. Have been for days, since all I can think about is your creamy flesh, or your soft hair." He tugged her head, gently this time. "All I want is to be inside you."

"Yes, please. Please," she begged.

His mouth latched onto her breast and sucked hard, sending a series of shivers down her arms and making goosebumps spring up. She couldn't take it anymore.

"Tucker," she pleaded.

"I don't think so, Maggie." His tone deepened, the dark warning a quick reminder she'd forgotten again to address him properly.

She breathed deeply. "Sir... It doesn't feel like enough. I — I don't know. Not intimate enough." Vaguely aware she sounded like a ridiculous adolescent she still couldn't let it go.

He pulled back and left her breast wet and aching, her surrounding flesh still on fire from his nips. "Maybe you should try Master."

Her body shuddered but he held fast and she

could not lift her head and look at his eyes no matter how much she struggled. Her eyes burned as a flood of emotion worked through her. It was too hard to think straight.

"M—Master," she tested the word on barely a breath.

"Fuck," Tucker swore and released her head. Maggie grabbed his shirt to keep from falling. "Shit, sorry." He curved an arm around her lower back and dove his other hand into his pocket. All the extra movement pressed his cock against her pussy, making her moan. Good gracious she needed him to be quick.

When he finished digging he lifted her slightly. "Scoot back a little on my knees, little one."

Maggie tried to accommodate his request, but there wasn't a hell of a lot of room in the back seat of his car. She glanced up and found Tucker unbuckling his belt and shoving his pants under his butt. Her mouth dropped open and saliva pooled. His shirt had come undone and the sculpted muscles underneath drew all of her attention. Especially the small trail of light brown hair from his navel that disappeared into his underwear.

There it was. The bulge of his desire practically staring her in the face. Long, thick and fucking big. Even the tip extended past the waistband of his briefs and she saw a drop of wetness she ached to lap up. She licked her lips.

"Maggie!"

Startled, she lost her balance and slipped from where she'd perched on the edge of Tucker's knees. In a flurry of hands and knees she fell sideways into the black hole of space between the rear bench and the back of the front seat. The sudden jolt sent a riot of sensations streaming through her as the plug moved inside her backside. Her eyes rolled to the back of her head.

"Oh shit. Maggie, are you all right?"

Before she managed to utter a word, he'd lifted her around the waist and pulled her next to him. His hands ran across every inch of her arms and legs before he stroked her face. When he finally seemed satisfied that she'd not broken anything he lifted his head and their gazes met. The look of shock she found sealed her fate. She lost it.

Her first laugh sounded like a snort and that made her laugh harder. She rolled to her side and wrapped her arms around her stomach as uncontrollable sounds bubbled out of her. "Oh my God. I fell on the floor. I'm trying to have the best sex of my life and I fell on the stupid floor of your car. Of all the ugly, ungraceful things that could have happened…"

She could tell from the sounds coming from Tucker that he was trying really hard to hold it in. "The best sex of your life?" He sounded incredulous.

She glanced at him then. "Well, yeah if it ever freaking happens." Suddenly feeling very exposed she crossed her arms over her breasts and clamped her lips shut to staunch her giggles. She refused to look at him again or she'd never get them under control. "You ever get the feeling this isn't supposed to happen between us? Like we're doomed or something?"

"Oh hell no, Maggie Cisco. Don't you dare go there. This is happening. *Right now*," he emphasized.

The sound of ripping paper caught her attention and she turned in his direction in time to see him pull his cock free from its underwear cage and roll a condom over his hard length. All the laughter inside died and every ounce of hunger she'd been fighting rushed forward.

"Come here." He grabbed her around the waist and lifted her again until he'd positioned her over his knees where the tip of his dick nudged at her hungry opening. "No more waiting. No more excuses. The only way you'll get me to stop now is to say your safe word."

She met his gaze and found the full extent of Tucker's truth. She was his and he was in charge. Her stomach fluttered. How was it possible for her to still be nervous considering everything he'd already done to her?

"Put your arms above my head on the top of the seat and don't move them until I give you permission, is that understood?"

"Yes...Master." Oh damn she loved the way that word sounded. So much more erotic than simply "Sir" and a far cry from Tucker, the boy she remembered from high school.

With her hovering just out of reach of her fondest desire, he pinched her nipples again, rolling them between his fingers with enough pressure to send sensation rioting through her.

"Take me, Maggie," he commanded.

With a wail that bordered on a scream, she sank onto his girth. Her eyes widened as her body tried to accommodate his full length with the plug already taking up most of the room. She panted for air.

"Take it easy. You can take it," he assured her, his hands wrapping around her bottom. "You're definitely tight, though."

A sheen of perspiration broke out across Maggie's skin. She breathed heavy against Tucker's neck. His fingers dug into her backside as the slow burn of desire stoked higher as she lowered inch by inch until she'd taken all of him.

"Good girl. Now fuck me." His hips jerked, beginning her slow drag back to the tip. White spots danced in her eyes and she swore she saw stars.

Tucker tried not to be affected by her tiny cries. He actually enjoyed the fact she wasn't a quiet submissive. But right now he needed to keep a level head or it would be over before they really got started. The waiting game he'd enforced on their relationship was now biting him in the ass.

With her body slick with sweat and the short ends of her hair flat against her face, she reminded him of a fairy sprite. A very naked, bouncy sprite with a cunt so hot she made him want to come into her. Despite the need to flip her over and pound into her, he managed to hold his hips still and let her give them pleasure. It probably never occurred to her that in this position her desire to make him happy took control. She would work to please him like a good submissive did.

Another fast drag of tight, wet heat made his insides quiver right along with her muscles. "That's it, little one. Fuck me hard. Rough."

A small scream erupted from her when he bent forward and gripped a nipple with his teeth. That bite of pain sent her into a frenzy as she pistoned faster, drawing closer to the ultimate release.

"You're mine, Maggie. Mine to play with as I please." Her pussy squeezed hard, signaling her approach to orgasm. It wasn't going to take much to send her over. "Isn't that right?"

She frantically nodded her head.

"Say it. Tell me who you belong to." He'd get the words before she came.

"You. My new Master." Another scream tore through her as the muscles of her pussy clamped down on his dick like a fucking vice on steroids. Her body jerked and Tucker used the momentum to force her hips up and down in savage strokes.

Between the sweet scent of sex and his need for

her wrapped around his balls, he had to come now. He shoved upward, pinning her hips to his and groaned. His release jetted into her taking with it all the pent-up need from his self imposed exile. She knew so little about the vileness of his past but none of that mattered now.

Maggie gave him hope. Sex with countless strangers had never filled the void his guilt had left behind, always leaving his psyche empty and battered afterward. Not this time. Maggie was it for him. The one. Whatever it took, he'd find a way to keep her.

The sounds of the road brought Tucker out of his head. As much as he intended to stay buried inside her for much of the night, they were almost home and she was about to remember they'd had an audience. A quick glance in the rear view mirror revealed no sign of his driver's reaction. His eyes were glued to the road as he'd expected.

As much as he planned to keep Maggie to himself, it gave him a jolt to know they'd been watched. A witness to his new submissive's wanton responses. Tucker smiled before lifting Maggie and rearranging her on the seat beside him. He tucked her hair behind her ears and wiped the sweat from her brow. Her eyes were closed but the flush of her cheeks and the still-rapid breathing indicated she was still very much in the moment.

"Open your eyes, Angel. I want to see you."

She shook her head. "I can't."

"Why not?"

"Because he was watching," she whispered.

Tucker glanced in the mirror and caught the driver's eye this time and the appreciation for the show practically glowed from his gaze.

The car came to a stop and Tucker finished fixing their clothes. Once he got Maggie situated, he reached into his wallet, pulled out a card and handed it across the seat. "Take this back to Purgatory and ask for Gabe. You'll be taken care of."

He reached across Maggie, opened the door and scooted them out.

"What was that all about?"

He smiled down at the love of his life. His perfect submissive. "You think after driving so well with so many distractions, the man doesn't deserve a bonus?"

It only took a second for the blush to turn her face bright red and then realization dawned. Tucker nodded. "That's right."

"You confuse me, Tucker Lewis."

Maggie took a step toward the house and he scooped her into his arms. "That's Master Tucker Lewis to you now. You can't take it back."

"I wouldn't dream of it…Master."

CHAPTER THIRTEEN

Tucker bemoaned giving his housekeeper the weekend off when the insistent person at his front door pressed the buzzer again. He grabbed his remote and tuned the television to his security channel. Not many people made personal visits without an appointment and he certainly wasn't up to a visit from his nosy sister.

His eyes widened at the image on the screen. That was definitely not his sister. He glanced to the other side of the bed where Maggie still slept. Her short hair spiked every which way and some of the makeup she'd worn the night before smudged below her eyes. And she looked more beautiful than ever. His gaze traveled along the curves of her body, stopping at her breasts where in the light of day he could see the many red marks he'd left behind when he nipped at her skin through the night.

His body tensed with want for her.

Reluctantly, he eased from the bed and the gorgeous submissive who'd be ready for him if he woke her. He preferred to pull her close and open her legs for a good morning kiss that would shock her awake. He sighed at the noise coming from outside the house. Not meant to be this morning. He dragged on pants and trudged to the front door. Through the glass he got a clear view of one of his closest childhood friends and a man he thought he'd never see again.

Mason Davenport stood tall and broad, exactly as he'd last seen him. He was built like a brick house and was the best damn linebacker because of it. It was kind of like looking in a mirror if he'd bulked up and grown out his hair.

Tucker entered his code into the security system that would unlock everything and yanked open the door. "Well, well. Talk about what the cat dragged in."

Mason grunted. "Yeah, it's good to see you too. Now let me in before my balls shrivel up and fall off out here. I forgot how damned cold winter is on the lake."

"You must be busy vacationing somewhere nice and warm." Tucker backed up and motioned for Mason to enter.

"Vacationing my ass. I wouldn't know what that was if it reached up and bit me."

"Surly as ever, I see." The humor he'd hoped to find in his friend's eyes simply wasn't there. Tucker sobered his thoughts for whatever coming storm Mason would deliver. "I'm surprised to see you."

"Not as surprised as I am to be here." Mason walked into the kitchen and headed to the coffeemaker like it'd been yesterday since he was last here, not five years ago. He poured two cups, added the perfect amount of sugar to the strong black coffee and handed off a mug to Tucker.

He grabbed the coffee and took a swig, ignoring the slight burn of the hot brew. "I'm having a moment of déjà vu here, Mason. What's going on?"

"Same old, Tuck. Paranoid as usual."

He put his mug down on the countertop and faced his friend. "You call it paranoid, I call it instinct, or whatever it takes to be prepared." He moved a little closer to his friend and lowered his voice. "You should know that I'm not alone this morning so our reunion will have to be short." He wasn't sure how he felt about seeing Mason after all these years and Maggie only complicated things. They'd made a pact to never look back and Mason's return brought a lot of tough memories to the surface he didn't want to rehash.

"I know. I've seen her."

That little nugget punched Tucker in the gut. "Exactly how long have you been hanging around before you decided to knock on my door?"

"Someone is digging into our past." Mason ignored Tucker's question. "Or more specifically someone is looking for the owner of Purgatory."

That stopped him cold. "Why the hell would someone do that? It's been years."

Mason shrugged. "I guess the current news isn't as salacious these days. Maybe someone is looking for a promotion. Hell, I don't know." He threaded his fingers through his hair. "A couple of months ago Gabe contacted me to let me know someone came in asking a lot of questions. I ignored it. Inquiries happen on a semi regular basis." He put his coffee down on the table. "Then about the time the same woman showed up at the club again, I heard about your Maggie's return. From everything you've told me about her, she's had a more interesting life than I would have expected."

"You can leave her out of this. I haven't told her anything…" He let the sentence hang between them because he knew that if he and Maggie grew closer he would eventually have to tell her everything.

"Yet."

Tucker didn't acknowledge him.

"When I got the call you'd rejoined the club I figured it was time to come home and find out what was going on."

Tucker didn't like the look in his friend's eyes. "Give me a break, Mason. I own part of the club so it's not unreasonable for me to show up every once in a while. Once every few years shouldn't cause any suspicions."

His friend shook his head. "We should have dumped the place years ago. It's never going to be the same. And if the truth comes out, everything we've done will be for nothing."

"That's a lot of drama you're slinging around at—" He checked the clock on the wall "—nine in the morning. You could have called, sent an email. I'm not sure you showing up here was a good call. We aren't kids anymore and maybe no one gives a shit anymore about a dead religious nut or his son."

"What about her?" Mason motioned toward the back of the house.

Anger rose sharp. "Don't."

"I have to. There's more at stake than just you and you damn well know it."

Now he was really getting pissed. "You think I don't know that?" He kept his tone level, hiding the anger. All he needed was for Maggie to come in and find him and Mason going at it. "I live here every day remember? I know exactly what's at stake."

"Maggie's return is either the worst case of timing or there's more going on. I don't believe in coincidences."

"And you call me paranoid? I doubt Maggie knows anything about what happened. Apparently when she leaves town she leaves everything." Tucker leaned against the wall and took a slow even breath before he continued. "She's submissive." The memory of her sweet responses and easy compliance simmered in his chest. She brought out all the need and longing he'd tried so hard to suppress and so far he got the impression their desires matched up pretty fucking well. "I don't want to deny who I am anymore. It's taken a long damn time to get here but I'm finally ready to accept it."

"So you know about the book she's writing?"

"What book?" The pit in Tucker's stomach grew hard. Maggie hadn't said a word about a book. They'd discussed some of her research but nothing beyond that.

"Christ, Tucker. You're fucking a woman who was arrested in a BDSM club, was recently one of the top nationwide scandals and she's supposedly writing some sort of memoir that you know nothing about? And you don't see anything wrong with this picture?"

Tucker clenched and unclenched his fist. "This is bullshit. Maggie's only guilty of being in the wrong place at the wrong time. That's something we, of all people, should understand perfectly. To top it off, her story was splashed across the internet for anyone with an electronic device to read."

Mason shook his head. "I read it." He began reciting some of the headlines. "Young, female college professor busted in BDSM club. Bondage professor lands in divorce court thanks to her secret life. Scandalized professor steps down from teaching amid public scandal. Oh and my personal favorite. Has Professor Cisco been reading *that* book?"

Tucker groaned. "If she hears you poking fun at her life, there is going to be hell to pay by both of us."

"I am not making fun of her, you idiot. Don't you realize how ridiculous and convenient this sounds? Did you even look past those stupid headlines? She may have come home to lick her wounds, but what has she really been doing these last two months. If she's writing a tell-all book then you're about to join her in the spotlight."

Tucker turned away from his oldest friend. Some of what Mason offered made sense. Except nothing about Maggie set off his radar. She was kind and loving with an eager attitude to explore her submissive side.

"C'mon, Tucker. What is going on? If she knows you own Purgatory what do you think will happen? We can't afford to get caught up in her desire to capitalize on her scandal."

"Enough." He'd had enough. "I'm the one sleeping with her. Not you. If she's not being honest with her intentions then it will be up to me to deal with it. It wouldn't be the first time and I doubt it will be the last."

Mason held up his hands in surrender. "I'd love nothing more than for you to find some happiness here, my friend. But not at the expense of all the others."

"Thanks for the warning."

Mason shrugged and headed for the front door. They'd said enough.

At the threshold of the door he turned back and met Tucker's gaze. "You're wrong about one thing."

"What's that?" He inwardly winced at his sarcasm.

"Someone does care about the son."

*

A long time after Mason had left, Tucker stood at the window overlooking the lake. He loved his home, but would he ever escape the horror that haunted him?

"Tucker?"

He turned to find Maggie standing in the doorway wearing only one of his shirts tossed over her shoulders with the front still unbuttoned. The rumpled sexy submissive looked fabulous on her.

"Well, well, Professor. All you need is a pair of glasses and I dare say you'd be this student's wet dream." He filed that nugget of information away for another day. He did love a good role play scene and she'd look damned sexy in a costume.

"I doubt that." She pushed her fingers through her hair, trying to comb the wild strands into place and only exceeded in making a bigger mess.

"Come," he motioned for her to move forward. Her immediate compliance once again warmed his heart if not for the touch of annoyance surging through him. "On you knees, little one." This time she looked at him with clear hesitation. He raised his brow as her only warning. Fortunately, she came to her senses and slid to the floor in a fairly graceful move.

"Good girl." He brushed the hair from her forehead before he trailed his fingers behind her ear and across her cheek. Her satiny-smooth skin beckoned him. He wanted to spend hours exploring every surface and crevice of her body. He'd experiment with different touches and watch her go from pale to pink and eventually red.

"Why would you doubt my assessment? Do you believe I'd say something I didn't mean?"

Her head dipped a fraction lower in obvious repentance. "No, Master."

Her easy use of the word Master slid through him like the comfort food he craved when life sucked, working as a balm to his frazzled nerves.

"I'm not much of a morning person and I usually wake up on the wrong side of the bed. Until I've had my coffee, that is."

He chuckled. He understood that feeling well. He'd woken more times than he could count feeling like the undead in desperate need of a caffeine jolt. Hazardous side effect for an artist who easily lost days to his work.

"So what you're saying is, tomorrow morning when I wake you up with my dick in your ass, I'd better tie you down first."

Maggie's head jerked up and her eyes widened with that deer in the headlights look he loved so much. "What?" she asked.

A slow smile spread across his face. "Waking you up in surprising ways is going to be my new favorite thing." He chuckled and pulled her to her feet. "First, I think I need to feed you. You're going to need your strength today."

"And coffee?"

"Yes, and coffee. C'mon it's already made."

She trailed behind him toward the kitchen. "Ooh, a man after my own heart. I love it."

She had no idea. "I thought it was supposed to be a man you captured through *his* stomach."

"Are you kidding? I love food. I think I'd have an affair with it if I could."

He stopped cold and she crashed into him. "Did you seriously just tempt me with food and sex?"

To his surprise her arms came around his waist and she slid her arms toward his groin. "I hadn't really thought about it. Guess I forgot who I was talking to. Clearly you can turn anything into a kinky scenario."

She gave his hardening cock a quick squeeze and then let go so she could sprint around him and run for the back of the house. "First one to the kitchen gets to go first," she yelled over her shoulder.

Tucker shook his head and took off after her. Yep, sweet with a wild streak. If nothing else, she'd keep him on his toes.

She made it to the kitchen first but he wasn't about to let a technicality stop him. He tackled her to the floor, turning his body to make sure she landed softly. Any bruises his submissive suffered from would be both intentional and consensual.

Before she could catch her breath, he kissed her hard. He engaged every item in his arsenal. Tongue, teeth and the emotion he normally safeguarded.

In the back of his head he still vaguely heard Mason's warning but for now he pushed it aside. If after the weekend he harbored any doubts then he'd confront the pretty professor himself.

He had an idea.

Tucker pulled from Maggie's arms and lifted her into his.

"What are you doing?"

"Whatever I want," he responded. He didn't have to go far. When he reached the big island in the middle of his kitchen he pushed everything out of his way before he laid Maggie out on the marble slab like an offering to a God. Her butt hit the cool surface and she made a gasp that made his heart beat faster. He wanted a lot more noise like that.

"It's too cold," she frowned.

"Not for long, Miss Maggie." He reached for the bottom of his shirt she wore and slid it under her back until it cleared her shoulders. Instead of removing it he chose to use it to bind her arms together over her head.

"Tucker, what about the coffee? I need caffeine." Her question came out on short pants.

"This is what you get when you decide to tease the big bad Dom," he replied. He ignored the scowl on her face, tracing his hands down her arms, over her breasts to the now slick spot between her legs.

"Open them for me."

Lucky for her she didn't pretend to not know what he meant. A second later she spread her legs and her pussy flowered opened before his eyes. On a low growl he grabbed her knees and slid them further apart. He couldn't resist the view of her slightly swollen clit protruding from its hood or the soft puffy lips of her cunt reminding him how well he'd used her the previous night.

"I'm definitely hungry for breakfast, but I've changed my mind on the menu." He licked his lips.

Her small whimper met his ears, making him glance up. No distress. He saw only desire on her face.

"Any problem with that?"

"No, Master. I'm all yours," her tone as serious as his intentions.

Maggie's heart beat so hard she was surprised it didn't echo through the room. Tucker's eyes had darkened moments before he bent to her core. She held her breath as his mouth hovered mere inches above her sex making her clench with greedy need. She'd learned enough about him to know he'd make her wait until he was good and ready before he fucked her. There'd likely be some torture involved first.

"Now be a good girl, keep your arms above your head and be still." Tucker lapped at her slit from top to bottom and she nearly shot off the counter. Every nerve ending ignited and fired. He delved deeper, forcing her to clench her fists to keep from grabbing him. He was too damn good at this.

"You taste amazing. Much better than the cinnamon roll I was planning on." Every deep rumble of his voice vibrated through her abdomen and straight to her clit.

"Wait." She half-heartedly struggled. "You have cinnamon rolls?"

A sharp smack landed on her thigh. "Naughty submissives don't get treats. They get fucked harder."

The stinging imprint of his hand mingled with his words, making her moan. She'd give up cinnamon rolls for the rest of her life for this. *Maybe*.

His hands grabbed her knees and pinned her legs open while his mouth worked over her pussy. Maggie sighed, smothering the twinge of embarrassment over how wet he'd made her. How was this possible? She had no hope of ever resisting this man. One look — one touch — one word — and she was ready to do anything he wanted.

The beginnings of a violent storm gathered in her center, pulling her taut as she grappled with her complete loss of control.

"You're going to make me come," she warned.

He lifted his head, cutting off the direct touch she ached for. "And I'm going to swallow every drop and then make you do it all over again."

His erotic threat pushed the tension inside her

to the breaking point. His wicked tongue circled the swelling flesh of her clit, bringing her dangerously close to the edge. She only needed a little more. Maggie arched her hips and tried to get him to just the right spot...

To her dismay he lifted away from her. "I have half a mind to flip you over and spank your ass red." He frowned and glanced around the room. "Don't move." Before she responded he crossed the room and disappeared around the corner.

Without his hands gripping her legs or his mouth on her body, some of the heat they'd generated began to cool. A shiver worked up her spine. Her mind wandered to all the things that had happened in her life to lead her here. She'd made so many mistakes and wasted so much time. The last thing she'd expected to find when she'd gone into hiding was someone like Tucker. She'd tried to build defenses to keep from getting into any more trouble and he'd shown up in her life with a wrecking ball, ready to knock down any barrier that might keep him out. She didn't quite understand why.

"That's some crazy hard thinking you must be doing."

Maggie gasped. She'd gotten so lost in her thoughts she'd failed to hear his return.

"What's going on up there?" Tucker tapped her forehead after he stepped between her thighs.

"Nothing important." She shrugged off the

lingering thoughts and looked down her body to see he'd gone to retrieve a condom. Her sex clenched at the sight.

"Unacceptable, little one," he grabbed her hips and pulled until her butt hovered over the edge. Then he lifted her legs and placed her heels over his shoulder. "That was a little bit deeper than not important. His fingers slid slowly through her labia before he started an easy, torturous circling around her clit. Heat blasted from her head to her toes as the cooling arousal enflamed every last nerve ending it touched.

"Ahhh," she moaned. How did he do this? The man had a magic touch or something.

"Now tell me what you were really thinking. Otherwise, I'll keep this up for a very long time."

"So not fair," she gasped.

"Definitely not," he agreed. "But neither is shutting me out. We have to communicate. Open up."

He didn't make it easy to concentrate on his words. Sensation layered upon sensation until her head threatened to explode all while his fingers worked her over without letting up. She wanted to come so badly and he purposely stroked her closer and closer without giving her the last little bit she needed to get there.

Frustrated as all get out she blurted out what he wanted to hear. "I was thinking about how I was supposed to stay out of trouble when I came home and I'm not. Things are as out of control as they were before."

His fingers froze. "You think you're in trouble."

Maggie didn't know whether to cry in frustration or scream at him for stopping. Fortunately she had enough sanity left to know the Dom in Tucker probably wouldn't reward her for screaming at him. "Not trouble like 'I'm going to get arrested or fired from my job' trouble. More like entangled trouble."

Tucker's brows lifted and she swore he started to smile before his eyes narrowed and he returned his full attention to the sweet spot between her legs. "It doesn't have to be trouble you know."

For a brief second his fingers grazed the top of her clit, giving her enough of a jolt to make goose bumps rise on her skin. "You're driving me—" she bit her lip to keep from begging.

"What? Don't stop. Say what you need to."

"Are all Doms this chatty during sex? I swear I must have missed that part in my research."

A sharp spear of pain struck Maggie as Tucker pinched her clit between two fingers. "I can definitely drag this out if I need to."

Unable to catch her breath right away, she simply clamped her lips shut and worked to stay her sarcasm. Sitting on the edge like this was much harder than she'd ever dreamed.

Tucker leaned forward and prodded her sex with the tip of his erection. Excitement flared inside her. Oh God. She was so close to getting what she wanted.

He dipped his head lower and gently kissed her. "Right here, right now you're mine." As his tongue pressed deep inside her mouth so did his cock into her pussy. He seemed to be in no hurry as he inched his way forward. Within seconds, her legs were shaking and her heart beat frantically. His hands stroked her hips and sides, creating another layer of friction to drive her insane.

"You're so beautiful," he whispered against her lips.

Maggie moaned and reached for him, wanting to crawl inside him. But she found her arms and hands still tangled in his shirt, trapped. He didn't give her much time to worry about whether to move. His mouth worked down her throat and chest until he captured a nipple between his teeth. But it was the suction he applied that left her writhing underneath him. He pulled on the tip at the same time he finally bottomed out inside her.

Her arousal made it easy for her to accommodate his size, but nothing relieved the ache to move. She was so full. Everything ached. If he didn't move soon she'd literally go out of her mind. There was only one way to fix this.

"Please, Master. Fuck me," She pleaded.

A dangerous growl rumbled in his chest. The rumbling sound seeped through to her bones, warming her from the inside out.

"Pushy little sub."

There wasn't a lot of heat to his words but her stomach still tumbled at being called a sub. Tucker liked to use a lot of pet names, all of which worked to make her feel special.

Please," she begged, while struggling to move her hips underneath the weight of his body.

"Mmm. I do love the sound of begging. You may soon learn that you should be careful what you wish for."

Seconds later he withdrew to the tip and then slammed home, her body jerked by the force. A shock of sensation speared through her. Both pain and pleasure took her breath away. Without giving her a moment to recover, Tucker repeated the harsh move. The sudden change of pace left Maggie unable to move or react. It became immediately apparent that her job was to take what her Dom offered as he hammered into her over and over again. Each stroke brushed her over-sensitized clit without getting close to the friction she needed to come. He really was planning to drive her mad.

She nearly cried in relief when he changed his angle and fucked over a second nerve-rich spot inside her. Her resulting cry exploded across the room.

"Oh hell, little one. Your muscles are squeezing me, tempting me to give in. Is that what you're hoping for?"

Hell yes! She wanted to answer him but her

brain wouldn't work her mouth other than for long, loud wails that she couldn't believe came from her. How was she supposed to think at all with him pounding her into the kitchen counter? Every hard stroke pushed her so damned close to the edge she had to fight to hold on.

"What are you waiting for, Miss Maggie? Your little cunt is begging for the orgasm. You keep denying it. Let go. Come."

Maggie screamed. His words had the same affect over her as a cannonball smashing into a building. Pieces of her went flying in every direction. Her muscles convulsed uncontrollably and she swore her toes literally curled. "Tucker," she moaned.

For a moment, time froze after his last thrust inside her. In a surreal almost out of body experience, she listened to her name fall repeatedly from his lips. Sweat glistened across the taut muscles of his arms and she imagined all of his muscles working equally hard. What would it feel like if he didn't wear a condom when he came? Her stomach clenched.

Maggie winced at her own thoughts. Just because Tucker enjoyed displaying a fair amount of possessiveness during sex, didn't mean either one of them were ready for anything too serious. Reading anything more into it than what she could physically see would not be smart. She'd done enough not smart things lately.

"Now that's what I call a breakfast of champions." Tucker withdrew from her body and began to clean up.

Maggie rolled her eyes. "That's the best line you could think of?"

His head swiveled sharply in her direction and for a second the look in his eyes pinned her in place. She wasn't sure what he would do next. She had a sudden vision of the big bad wolf in her mind, then a smile broke out across his face and she heaved a sigh of relief.

"Such a smarty pants you are." He returned to between her legs with a warm cloth he'd retrieved from the sink and proceeded to clean her.

With the excitement of sex cooling off, the weight of embarrassment pressed down on her. She was still sprawled out across his kitchen counter with every inch of her body exposed and vulnerable. She struggled to sit.

"Not yet." He pressed a hand to her torso and pinned her back in place. "I'll let you know when it's time to move. For now let me finish taking care of you."

"But—"

His eyebrows rose again, "You enjoy arguing don't you? Sure you ended up in the right profession?"

Maggie forced herself to lie back and relax and think of anything other than the gorgeous hunk of man between her legs studying her more intently than her gynecologist did.

"Obviously not," she admitted. "I never really loved teaching as much as I loved my research and until the University asked me to leave, I assumed I'd found my calling."

"That's a mighty powerful "but" hanging in the air. How do you feel now?" He discarded the cloth and began a slow and easy massage of her thighs.

"Things are quite a mess. I had to go into hiding to escape the wrath of a few obsessed reporters, I doubt any University would take me on after the scandal, which isn't nearly as bad as I thought it would be." She took a deep breath. "I thought I'd miss everything being a professor entails…"

"But you don't."

There was a lot of sadness with that realization. "My entire adult life up to this point has revolved around the University in one way or another. I used to enjoy the rules and rigidity of being a student, then a teacher and then even married to a fellow professor."

His magic fingers continued its path along her entire body until he reached her arms and hands. First, he freed her from the entangled fabric of his shirt, then he returned to the delicious massage that had her muscles melting into the table.

"The submissive in you loved all those rules."

Her body went rigid at the implication of his words. "Relax. No one is judging you. It's not uncommon for many submissives to find themselves in jobs where rules and protocols dictate much of their lives. It's nothing to be ashamed of."

Maggie wasn't sure about his analysis. Where were the facts and figures to support it?

"C'mon. You're about to undo all the hard work I just did." He scooped her from the island and headed toward the door.

"Wait. What are you—?" He bent at the knees to grab the door handle. "No, I don't want to go outside. Without my clothes I'll freeze to death!" she cried.

Tucker shook his head. "Ye of little faith." Despite her protests, he pushed open the glass door that led to the back deck and stepped out of warm safety of the house.

Maggie grit her teeth against the impending cold, waiting for the blast to take her breath away. The sudden change in temperature she expected never came. Instead of an outdoor deck like she'd assumed, she now realized the entire area was enclosed by glass and judging by the lack of freezing temperatures, climate controlled.

"You could have told me you had a sunroom where I wouldn't freeze my ass off," she huffed.

"Where would the fun be in that? Watching you panic and squirm was way more fun."

Maggie frowned at him. "Oohh… At the risk of sounding like a broken record, you really are mean."

Without breaking stride, or putting her down, Tucker stepped down the stairs into a steamy hidden hot tub. He sank down into the heated water taking her with him.

"Holy—" she gasped. The hot water temporarily scorched her skin. Not enough to make her want out, but enough to take her breath away until her body adjusted to the sudden increase in temperature.

"Your skin is already pinking up," he observed, touching her arm gently. "Is it too hot for you? I tend keep it extremely hot. It's my preference. He placed her down on to one of the built in curved seats and turned and stepped out of the tub.

Faced with his retreating back, she blurted, "Don't leave me."

He paused, turning back to her. "I'm definitely not leaving. Just grabbing some necessary supplies. Lie back and relax, let the heat do its magic. You need to recover for later." He winked and headed back into the house.

His naked backside walking away was a treat to behold. He had a butt sculpted to perfection on top of long tan legs with a healthy sprinkling of dark brown hair. Her stomach fluttered. She loved the way the hair on his arms and legs felt when he slid over her skin. Soft and rough at the same time. Maggie sighed when he disappeared out of sight, sinking back into the comfy seat.

Despite what he said, she was definitely in trouble here. She laid her head back on the tiled edge and looked up at the impossibly blue Carolina sky. It would be too damned easy to get used to this. She didn't really understand much about Tucker's life anymore than she did her own.

She had a feeling he was far more than a patron at Purgatory and wouldn't be surprised to learn he was more involved with the club than he'd let on. That new thought unsettled her. Given time it was certainly possible she'd want to go back, but not for a while. She'd need more time to be ready. That would likely put a pretty big crimp in his style. Although she'd heard more than one comment about how long it had been since he'd been there. Maggie made a mental note to ask him about that.

"Falling asleep in there?" Tucker's deep voice permeated the fog of Maggie's brain.

"I'm thinking about it."

She heard Tucker enter the hot tub and take a seat next to hers. "You might want to wait until you've had one of these first."

She took a deep breath, ready to tell him whatever it was it could wait when the scent of cinnamon and sugar drifted through her brain. "Oh. My. God. Is that..." She cracked an eye open to find a plate of cinnamon rolls shoved under nose. "It is."

She sat up and grabbed one, stuffing it in her mouth in two seconds flat.

"Sexy," he drawled.

Maggie shrugged mid chew. He'd discovered her weakness. "Nothing gets between me and a cinnamon roll. They're my favorite."

"Good to know." He sat back and relaxed. She watched him rotate his shoulders and move his head side to side.

"Sore muscles?" she asked. Maggie popped the last bite of her delicious sweet roll into her mouth and scooted closer to Tucker. "Turn around."

One of his eyebrows climbed.

Maggie ignored the look and climbed behind him in the tub. She curled her legs around his hips and snuggled comfortably so she could massage his shoulders and back. Faced with the up close view of his muscles, she tried to ignore the tingle in her breasts and pussy. Her visceral reaction aside, she wanted to give something back to him.

"Have you slept much this week?" she asked.

He grunted some non-committal sound as her fingers went to work on his shoulders. "Sleep is overrated. Isn't that what they say?"

"I guess," she answered. As she kneaded his muscles loose her mind wandered back to high school and the boy who'd stolen a kiss from her. He'd scared her witless when he'd pulled a reaction so fierce from her that she'd been numb for days afterward. Even now, all these years later, her body still came alive when she remembered the feel of his mouth on hers.

He'd become her secret crush for years. The unrequited lust she never quite got over. After she'd left for college she moved on but somewhere in the back of her mind, she knew that it was that one kiss that set the standard for every man who came after him.

"What happened to you after high school?" she blurted. There was so much she didn't know and it was time to fill in the blanks.

His back stiffened, the move so slight if she hadn't been touching him she'd likely not have noticed. A few seconds ticked by without an answer. Finally he sighed and the muscles underneath her hands relaxed a fraction.

"Same as you. I went off to college. Although I didn't go far. I opted for football at East Carolina."

Maggie frowned. "You'd think I would have heard about one of our own becoming a college football star."

A deep rumble of laughter from Tucker made her smile. "You give me too much credit. The whole football thing ended up not working out."

"I find that hard to believe. I remember you were quite the superstar in high school."

"Things change when you least expect it." His voice lowered to a soft cadence.

She hoped that meant he was starting to relax. "So what happened to derail your plans? Did you meet a woman in college?"

"I met many women in college. It's where I truly discovered my interest in BDSM. It was certainly an eye-opening experience. But when my dad died I had to come home and take care of my family."

Her hands stilled on his back. Smooth move, idiot. She vaguely remembered something about his dad dying. House fire, she thought.

"I'm sorry, I didn't mean to dredge up bad memories."

He grabbed her right hand and turned back to her. "You have nothing to be sorry for, little one. It's only natural for you to be curious about your new Dom."

A sudden burst of butterflies took flight in her stomach. He kept referring to her as his, or calling himself her Dom. And she still wasn't sure how to take it.

Tucker smiled. "You should see your face when you worry. It's so adorable." He touched her brow and brushed his fingers back and forth across her skin. "Do you ever take anything at face value or do you attempt to analyze everything?"

Maggie sat back in her seat and grabbed the glass of orange juice he'd left for her on the tray. "Old habits I guess. It's who I am. I live for facts and data."

Tucker leaned forward and licked the orange juice from her lip. "Here's a fact for you. Very soon, I'm going to bend you over, hold you down and fuck you till you can't walk."

Her eyes widened and her body went on alert. Thankfully, the frothing water covered her erect nipples from his gaze. Her chest constricted, forcing her to open her mouth to take in more air.

"Beautiful," he exclaimed before he swooped in and kissed her hard. His tongue thrust inside and roughly tangled with hers. An edge of need exploded inside her. One minute they were having a casual conversation and the next he'd turned it around and began taking what he wanted. Never in her life had she felt so desired, even cherished.

He had a way of dominating their time together that made her want nothing more than to give him everything. He tumbled her further into the water until the long length of his erection prodded her belly. He made it so easy to let go...

Tucker turned Maggie in his arms and continued to kiss her at random intervals. At this angle he easily pushed two fingers inside her. The water from the hot tub wasn't the only thing keeping her wet. He stifled a groan against her neck. She would be the death of him if he wasn't careful. He realized remaining calm was an impossible goal when he felt his cock pulse against her soft skin.

Screw this. "C'mon." Tucker lifted her from the water and carried her to the nearby lounge chair where he'd be able to lay her out, watch the sun glow across her skin and fuck them both into oblivion.

There simply was no getting enough of his Maggie...

CHAPTER FOURTEEN

Tucker stared down at the woman hunched over in the corner of the garden room. The plush chair enveloped her, making her look more fragile than ever. He'd stood here for at least an hour hoping to gain a response from her but like the other hundreds of times he'd visited her, she refused to look at him or utter a sound. At a time like this he found it almost impossible to remember the mother he'd once had. She'd been so vibrant and loving with the whole world at her feet, including him.

He wasn't above admitting how much of a mama's boy he'd been growing up. He'd lived with a hard, unyielding father who constantly rode his ass and his mother's beauty and grace balanced that.

Until the fateful night his entire world had come crashing down. He often wondered what would have happened if he, Mason and Levi had not decided to head to his house for a long weekend that day.

"Mr. Lewis. Visiting hours are over." A nurse spoke softly behind him. They often gave him a lot of leeway, but if they were urging him to go now then it was truly time for him to leave. "You've certainly done your best by your mother, Sir. Sometimes it's just easier for patients to not face the pain inside them."

He winced at the nurses' words. He knew they were meant to comfort and soothe, but they had the opposite effect on him. Of course, she had no idea how awful the truth really was. It didn't surprise him that his beautiful mother had chosen to withdraw from life. Hell, he'd followed the same path for a while. Except he'd hidden at home more often than not with a bottle of alcohol and a parade of warm bodies to keep him company. If not for his stubborn sister he could have easily fallen into the same pit as his mother.

Nina was an incredible woman, who'd endured far worse, and he discovered pretty quickly that they were each other's rocks. With the loss of Levi and Mason from their lives, they'd each found their own path of recovery. She'd put all of her energy and effort into her business, which now thrived, and he'd burned through the betrayal and loss with glass and a hot furnace.

Maggie's return had been the final wake up call. He'd eagerly anticipated their inevitable reunion while spending those last weeks putting his life into an order that made sense. Business was still business but he spent a small fortune each month on the right people to run it for him, while he did his level best to stay out of the spotlight. None of them could afford to draw attention too close. He glanced again at his mother. There were so many things he wished for her that were completely out of his control.

His father's death had resulted from the worst night of their lives and no amount of pleading and promising got through to her. He'd tried it all. She wasn't even Nina's mother and he'd watched his sister hold her hand and promise her that everything would be fine if she came back to her son. That what she'd endured meant nothing compared to a family's love.

Tucker pushed off the wall he'd let hold him up. Weariness weighed him down as usual. He'd go, since there was nothing he could do here. Of course, that wouldn't stop him from returning next week and trying all over again.

He turned and touched the kind nurses' shoulder. "Thank you, Bessie. You've been so kind to our family I wish you'd let me repay you."

Tears shimmered in the woman's eyes. "There is nothing to repay. Your mother has a beautiful soul and it is a privilege to care for her."

He grimaced. "How can you tell? She's never spoken to you."

"It doesn't take words to read a person Mr. Lewis. Just like I see you standing here for hours every week watching over her, I see the look in her eyes when you arrive. She loves you more than words can say."

The bitter pill of the nurse's statement lodged in his throat. If his mother were still present and emotionally aware then why the hell wouldn't she speak to him? They could have gotten through this together.

Tucker had to fight the urge to put his fist through something. It was time to say goodbye before he did something stupid. He strode over to his mother's chair and leaned down to press a kiss to her temple. "Love you, mom. I'll see you next Sunday. Wish me luck this week. If things work out the way I want I may have a surprise for you when I return." To his infernal dismay, his words had no affect on her. She sat perfectly motionless with her eyes staring straight ahead out the window.

He lifted his head and followed her line of sight. The winter landscape wasn't the most appealing but his mother could sit and overlook the water from either the solarium or her room. He'd made sure that was an option for her. All her life she'd wanted to be as close to water as possible. The large man-made lake might not be ideal but it served its purpose as she sat here in front of the window all day, every day thinking who knew what.

Satisfied that his mother was well taken care of and that he'd see her again in seven days, he gently squeezed her thin shoulder and walked out. On autopilot he moved through the visitors center and out into the parking lot. He'd been fortunate that the Rose Park Center was not only one of the highest-rated treatment facilities for mental health, it also only took him a couple of hours drive to reach it.

Today he needed every minute of that drive to shake off the weight of his mother's condition before he returned home. Well, not exactly his home. He'd taken Maggie to her parents cabin early this morning with the promise he'd be back as soon as possible. He preferred sooner rather than later. His choice had been for her to wait for him at his house but she'd insisted on going home. In the face of his refusal to elaborate on his errand, her excuse to retrieve some clothes and personal items rang hollow. She also didn't seem to believe him that there would be no need for any clothing today. His house, his rules.

They hadn't even made their way back to the playroom. There were so many things he had in mind to do to her there. Not that his bedroom wasn't adequately equipped. Tucker slid into the back seat of his car and nodded for his driver to go. Maggie didn't know it, but having her in his life made some of the dark shadows infinitely lighter. She had a smile that tempted even the coldest heart to thaw and the look of a sprite with unkempt hair who had an inquisitive mind bound to get her in trouble again. And curves made for sin… He adjusted his pants to make more room in the crotch and blew out a hard breath. It was damned difficult to think about Maggie and not get hard.

From the moment he'd received the fateful call

from his sister that she'd returned, Maggie had never been far from his mind. Some of what he'd lost came back that day. The legacy of his father had fractured so many lives it had taken many of them years to recover. Maggie back in his life made him want to move on and start really living again.

He closed his eyes and laid his head back on the seat and imagined his little sub in the hot tub the morning before. She'd been such a delight his cheeks still hurt from smiling. So many of her reactions spoke of innocence. Not the "Ooh I'm a virgin" kind of innocence, he thought. More like the "I'm not jaded" kind.

He hesitated, remembering Mason's very real warnings barely twenty-four hours before. He ignored the perpetual knot in his stomach. Mason was right about one thing. He'd let paranoia rule him for far too long. For the first time in a very long time, his instincts told him that Maggie was not like the others and could care less about his money or his secrets. Life had not been easy for her and it was her turn to be taken care of. As far as he could tell she'd given everything she could to her marriage and career and then had the rug ripped out from under her. The pain in her heart was something she'd live with for quite a while.

Tucker grit his teeth against the burning behind his eyes. The thought of hurting Maggie made his chest tighten and his gut burn. A woman like her deserved to be cherished.

Her ex husband must have been an idiot. However, he was not. It was time to take the next step with Maggie. Right after one more stop…

* * *

Maggie opened her front door with a smile on her face and not a damn thing else. Faced with a willing and gorgeous woman who tugged at him in ways he didn't quite know how to express, he immediately forgot about the "talk" he'd planned. Instead she'd triggered the Dom who desperately needed to connect with his enchanting submissive.

Her smile died and concerned etched across her lovely face. "What's wrong?"

"This is definitely not what I'd expected." His voice lowered and vibrated with the desire already tugging at his groin. "Not that I'm complaining," he clarified.

He stepped through the door and closed it behind him. "However, if you're going to greet me in the nude I'd much prefer to see you waiting in a submissive pose. On you knees, little one."

Maggie frowned and stared at him. He read the concern and the unanswered questions that would have to wait until later. He wasn't ready to talk about it. "Not now. Trust me."

Her internal war continued for a few seconds longer before she bit her lip, lowered her eyes and sank to the ground as instructed. Tucker pushed the box he'd been holding into his jacket pocket before he removed the coat and draped it across one of her living room chairs. He stood back and studied every inch of her. She was a pretty woman but naked and on her knees she took his breath away. He stepped forward and touched her hair, smiling with deep satisfaction when she relaxed her posture under his hand.

"I'd ask what you've been up to today, but doubt that's what either of us wants right now. You've honored me with your openness and I plan to take full advantage of it."

"I'm yours, Master," she spoke quietly.

"Yes, you are. Now stand and undress me." The thought of her hands touching him made him harder. He'd been right about one thing. A short-term fling with Maggie would never be enough. Tonight he'd convince her that she needed him as much as he needed her. Teaching her about D/s had started out as a great idea in his head but he'd known almost from the moment he touched her that she'd irrevocably change him. She'd made him incessantly hungry for more.

As she stood, he reached for a breast and began plucking at her nipples. "It's a shame I don't carry nipple clamps. These beauties look incredible clamped and tied."

She raised her face. "I have some."

Tucker worked hard not to let his mouth drop open. "Mmm." He pinched a puckered tip particularly hard. "Such a surprise you are." He dropped his hands and nodded his head. "Go get them then. Hurry, Maggie. I'm not feeling particularly patient today."

She spun and ran for the back of the cabin. To facilitate the coming scene, Tucker unbuttoned his shirt and removed his belt.

His little sub returned and held up more than simple nipple clamps. No his Maggie, had clamps connected by a chain which then attached to a dark purple and black thick leather collar. He stared at the items in his hand. "Have you worn this before? Who bought it for you?"

A nervous look crossed her face and those adorable teeth nibbled on her lip again. "I bought it. I thought I could get an idea of what it felt like to experience some pain without a spanking and I'd get a chance to feel the weight of a collar around my neck. For research," she added.

Uh. Huh. Research. Poor little sub wanted it so bad she tried it out by herself. That put a picture of her spread out in bed with the clamps and collar restricting her as she masturbated. He wiped his eyes and shook his head. "Show me."

"What?" He watched her eyes open wide.

"You heard me. You're mine to do with as I wish tonight and I wish to see exactly how you played with this. *Right now.*" He'd sharpened his voice, giving her no choice but to comply.

Maggie's hands fidgeted with the collar until she got the buckle undone. With slow and slightly jerky moves, she placed the collar around her neck. Tucker moved behind her and helped her fasten the thick and supple leather. Not exactly what he'd had in mind, but fuck if she didn't look hot like this.

He spun her around to face him again, pulling her close to briefly grind his cock against her mound. "Keep going."

Her mouth opened on a pant but her hands moved of their own volition. She lifted one dark clamp and loosened the side screw before she squeezed the clip onto one of her tight, dusky nipples. The harsh breath that huffed from her gorgeous mouth went straight to his already straining dick.

Fortunately for them both, she hurriedly attached the other one as Tucker strained not to bend her over and shove his cock in her pussy where they stood. It had taken some time for him to get his groove back, but it was there now. The Dominant in him needed to take…

With both tits pinned, Maggie groaned.

"You like that bite of pain don't you?" From the moment she'd expressed her distaste for spanking, he'd pushed against her misconceptions in regards to various forms of pain. He didn't need her to love the act of spanking as much as he did, he only needed her not to hate or fear it. Since he loved to spank a pretty sub's ass, he'd happily reserve that act for when she'd earned a punishment. Something they'd need to address fairly soon.

Her eyes lifted and met his. "I never really thought I would," she admitted.

"It's nothing to be ashamed of Maggie. Nor is being wrong about something shameful. We all make mistakes."

He reached for the pressure screws on the clamps and gave them a quarter clockwise turn.

Maggie gasped. "Fuck."

"Mmm. Such a perfect word from a saucy little mouth." He reached out and cupped her breasts. They filled his hands to perfection and he simply couldn't get enough of them. Or anything else about her. He flicked the tip of a clamped nipple and inwardly sighed at the lovely pants coming from his little Miss Maggie. This was how her body was meant to be decorated. Although later it would be his collar wrapped around her neck, not one she'd purchased on her own.

"Who do you belong to, Maggie?" He wanted so much to hear it from her.

"You, Master. I belong to you."

He ran his fingers around both breasts before taking one finger further down her chest and belly. He swirled it in her belly button and imagined how incredible she'd look with a simple decorative stud here that his tongue could play with as he worshipped her body on a nightly basis. After she accepted his collar she would without question be his to do as pleased. He continued past the swell of her belly and dipped toward her soft pussy.

"Do you wish to truly belong to me, Maggie?"

Her eyes widened and a sheen of tears glossed over her eyes. "I really do," she whispered. "More than anything else."

Her heartfelt words tugged at his heart. If he hadn't already been falling in love with her...

Claim her.

The words kept reappearing in his mind like a continual chant. He steeled against the driving desire and focused on what Maggie needed. He dipped his hand lower and between her soaked folds. She was ready for him. He circled her clit over and over being careful not to get too close to the bundle of nerves that would set her off. He wasn't ready for her to go there yet.

Tucker bent forward and grasped the chain running between her breasts with his teeth and straightened to his full height. Maggie groaned when the chain pulled taut and the pain in her tits sharpened. Her eyes widened and her mouth opened to the perfect O.

"Do you want to serve me as my submissive?"

She frantically nodded.

He growled his disapproval.

"Sorry. I cant—uhh—hard to think straight."

"That's my girl. Now answer the question," he insisted, pulling harder on the chain.

"Yes, Sir. Please. Let me serve you."

He loved the breathy sound of her voice. She'd

quickly gone from playful to submissive as need drove her to the edge.

"That depends on what you want to do for me."

"Anything you want, Sir. Anything," she repeated.

His chest tightened. He held so much pride for his lush and beautiful Maggie. Her open heart and willingness to learn and accept astounded him. It seemed wrong to subject her to the darkness in his life. Not that he had an ounce of willpower to walk away now. Although tonight she'd have to find out exactly what she was getting into. He wouldn't put a collar around her neck until she understood exactly what his genetics were capable of. It was certainly something that could mar their future.

Right now he was her Dom and she had needs that had to be fulfilled. Confession would come later and he prayed it truly was good for the soul. He couldn't fathom his future without her.

He left behind the swollen jewel of her clit and moved to the heated opening of her glorious pussy and the slick juices that awaited him. "I bet you'd like to come right about now."

Her legs quivered against his hand. "Yes, Sir."

He moved closer so his chest brushed her clamped tits. "Not yet, pet. Soon though." He dipped past her opening and circled the small bud of her ass instead. "I'm going to have you here tonight. I've made it my goal and you know how I am when I set goals."

She whimpered and sagged against him. From the slight tremor of her body he gauged she sat on the edge right next to him. He'd thought to take his time and hold her here for a while but his cock wanted her right now.

"On your back on the couch. Now Maggie."

He swore he saw relief on her face before she turned to do as he'd asked. The curve of her ass as she crossed the room beckoned him. There were half a dozen different ways he wanted to take her all pushing at his brain. And if she twitched that glorious ass at him one more time she was going to find herself on the floor face down getting her ass reamed six ways to Sunday.

Once she got into position he crossed over to her and maneuvered between her legs. "Raise your arms over your head and fold your knees up, baby." He pushed her legs high and wide, opening her pussy to his view. Her sex glistened with her arousal. He particularly loved how wet she got for him.

"Now tell me what you want, Maggie. I need the words." He slid his fingers between the lips of her cunt and parted her labia. "So pretty." He continued to play, teasing her clit and going so far as to push a single digit halfway into her tight little asshole.

"You aren't telling me, little one. Are you not ready?" He knew just the thing to get what he wanted from her. With one hand he rubbed her clit and with the other he removed one of the clamps on her nipple.

Maggie groaned and thrashed against his hand, doing everything she could to get more from him. Poor baby. He gently rubbed her sore nipple before he grasped the other clamp and removed it too.

This time Maggie rewarded him with a loud half grunt, half scream. "Tucker, please."

"Tucker is it?" He pinched the clit he'd so lovingly stroked.

"Master," she gasped.

"Much better." With her tits probably still on fire and her clit aching, he pushed a finger inside her and immediately stroked over the soft spot he already knew she loved. Her eyes rolled back in her head and her hips bucked in an attempt to get more. With his left hand he pushed down on her leg, while his thighs bracketed her hips, holding her in place. It wasn't quite the same as tying her down but the constant pressure from his grip would serve as an ever-present reminder that he was restraining her.

"Please. Master."

Two lovely words he would never get tired of hearing from her.

"More. Please. Need more."

"I know, baby. Just say it."

"Fuck me," she wailed.

"See that wasn't so hard." He lined his cock up with her opening and shoved forward into her pussy. Both hands tightened on her thighs, making sure she couldn't move. Her sex clenched around him and Tucker lost it. He pounded into her, holding nothing back. The time for gentle and loving would come another day when she hadn't tempted his control to the breaking point.

He thrust in and pulled out while battling the inner muscles she clamped down on him. Her lower body couldn't exactly move, yet Maggie had still found a way to play with him. He groaned and slammed harder. The stress and fear of his past began to burn away. This is what he'd needed all day. Being inside Maggie, feeling the connection between them. With her it wasn't just about sex. It was more elemental than that. She touched him on an emotional level. Her complete and utter submission went through him like a healing balm, taking away the anguish he fought to keep at bay.

He fucked her for a long time like this. No words were needed. Contentment came from the sounds she made when he hit her sweet spot or when the smack of flesh on flesh reverberated through the room.

Maggie's constant cries reached deep inside him and squeezed. She was part of him now. He wanted to give her so much more. He pressed his hand between them, rubbing his fingers repeatedly across the bundle of nerves that would set her off.

Her first orgasm nearly destroyed him, and the second sent him spinning out of control. His balls drew up. This was it. He shoved deep as far as he could go and fused their bodies together, groaning as come spurted from his dick. Tucker fell against her, pressing her into the sofa. What had she done to him?

He wrapped his arms around her soft body at the same time her legs wrapped around his waist. The smell of sex and sweat mingled with the sweet scent of Maggie. He nuzzled her air and drew in a deep breath. He'd forever associate fruit with sex thanks to her.

Tucker shifted and rolled until he was the one on his back and Maggie sprawled across his chest. He listened to her breathing return to normal and eventually slow down. He rubbed his fingers up and down the curve of her spine, reluctant to stop touching her. He needed to carry her to the bedroom and get her comfortable before they both fell asleep. But he really liked the feel of her weight pressing down on him. Maybe they'd stay like this a while.

"What happened today?" Her question came out on a soft sleepy whisper.

"Not yet, little one. Rest now and later we'll talk." To his horror his voice broke on the last. An hour or two more of being her white knight couldn't hurt.

"I think I'm falling in love with you."

The words were spoken so casually and light he almost missed them. For a moment guilt and happiness dueled inside him. As quickly as the joy grew, the unspoken truths between them washed it away. He had to tell her soon.

He waited for her to say something more but she didn't. Her breathing turned deeper and minutes later she began to snore. A light adorable sound that made him think of a kitten.

More like a big curvy cat with sharp razor nails. The smile that tilted his lips came as a shock. He pressed a kiss to her hair and whispered, "I love you too, little one."

* * *

Sated but restless, Tucker wandered through the darkness in Maggie's cabin. After several fun filled hours, he'd made Maggie come no less than a half dozen times. God, there wasn't enough sunshine in the world to give him the same amount of light as the look on her face when she screamed his name. With her hair plastered to her face by sweat, her body decorated with marks he'd given her and his cock deep inside her, she was the most gorgeous creature he'd ever met. And she was his.

He'd retrieve the collar he planned to present her and rejoin her in bed for another round. He still had a virgin ass to conquer.

Tucker glanced at the dying embers in the fireplace and considered restarting the fire. Considering how much heat he and Maggie managed to generate on their own, he decided they'd be fine the rest of the night without it.

He grabbed his jacket and lifted the long jewelry box from the inside pocket. She'd managed to derail his original plans when he'd arrived to find her naked and ready. Not that he'd minded. Her submission had blown his mind and then some. He casually surveyed her living space and its basic furnishings. Her parents left her a nice place, but there were several times throughout the day he'd wished they were in his fully-stocked playroom. He looked forward to getting her to agree to move in with him, the sooner the better as far as he was concerned.

On the opposite side of the door on the small desk he'd failed to notice earlier in the day, he spied what had to be her makeshift office. A thin silver laptop sat open and piles of notes and notebooks were haphazardly strewn across every inch of the surface. His gut tightened.

Don't go there, man.

Too late. His brain had already conjured Mason's warnings once again. *She's writing a book.*

Of course she was. Her research was her life. She'd offered him that information on several occasions and he'd read some of her papers online before they'd reconnected. To expect her to drop it the minute she left her job seemed ridiculous. Part of the reasoning he'd used to become her Dom had been so she could continue her work with real working knowledge.

Yet Mason's warning wouldn't leave him alone. All the rationalization in the world couldn't erase the seeds of doubt his friend had planted. He'd simply have to find out for himself what his little sub was up to so he could put all their fears aside. Later he'd really enjoy taking Mason down a peg or two for feeding into his former paranoia.

With every step Tucker took toward that laptop the pit in his stomach ached worse. He didn't relish invading Maggie's privacy. He should march into the bedroom and ask for the answers he sought. His feet stayed on their current path and he stopped short of her desk. The computer was still on and had likely gone into sleep mode after he'd arrived.

He tapped the mouse and watched the slim device come to life. Moments later a word document appeared on the screen and the word *memoir* flashed at the top like a god damned neon sign. Tucker took a deep breath and scrolled to the beginning. There were a lot of side notes already marked in different colors that stood out. Things like "research this info better" and "add more depth to this later".

He easily imagined her sitting here with glasses perched on top of her head and her hair standing on end from pulling it in frustration as she worked. He'd have to make her write some while he watched. He'd study every facet of his submissive like she studied BDSM. Then he'd bend her over the desk and fuck her until they both exploded.

His name on a page caught his attention and

pulled him from the fantasies he'd been planning to act out. About halfway through what she'd written his name came up. For a half a second he thought about simply walking away. Her work was none of his business.

Tucker sighed. That might be true if there wasn't so much at stake. Page by page he scrolled through everything she'd written, only to discover every single detail of their encounters had been transcribed in vivid detail. The bondage wheel, the club, his house, the hot tub. Every minute they'd been together had been added to her memoir in depth. Apparently when she wrote a book about herself she went all in.

At the point where she'd left off there were some sidebar notes again with questions. One in particular stood out among the others. *"Why would Tucker hide the fact that he owned the Purgatory club?"*

His blood ran cold at the sight of that one line. He'd never actually told her that nugget of information. He'd planned to, but not until he'd bound her to him with his collar.

This couldn't be happening again.

"Tucker, what's going on?" She'd snuck up behind him without a sound.

"Isn't that supposed to be my question? What the hell, Maggie? What is this? You've decided to share the intimate details of our relationship with the whole world without even checking first if I'd mind? Are you insane?"

He stood from her chair and whirled on her. She'd wrapped a small robe around her shoulders but still looked like the sex-ravaged nymph he'd left in bed.

"You went through my stuff?" The shell-shocked look on her face only served to piss him off more.

"That's not the point." He waved off the fact he'd invaded her privacy. "That's not a fucking research paper, Maggie. That's a tell all book and from the looks of it you plan to literally tell it all in dirty vivid detail."

"You don't understand." She clasped the robe together covering her naked body from his view. "When I first came back home I was pissed and sick to death of being vilified in the media. It was the only thing I could think of to fight back."

"And never mind who you hurt in the process." He wanted to kick himself when the anger deflated on Maggie's face and a look of defeat crossed it instead.

"So that's it. You're just another judge, jury and executioner out to crucify me without knowing shit about the truth." She turned away. "I can't believe this is what you assume of me after this week? No trust. No love. Only accusations. That's rich, Tucker. Although why I'm surprised I'll never know. You can join the lets beat up Maggie club if that's what you want, but you can damn well do it on the way out the door. Get out."

He grabbed her wrist and pulled her close. "Don't try to turn this on me. I wasn't the one planning to turn your life into a three ring circus."

Her head bowed. "My life already is."

"A relationship like ours has to be built on trust. Without that we have nothing."

Her body jerked as if he'd struck her. Somewhere in the back of his head a voice told him he'd gone too far. That is was time to stop and get out while he still could. Unfortunately, he didn't heed his own advice.

"You lied, Maggie. I thought I could trust you. Although I still don't get it. What's in it for you? Money? Did you plan on selling the book to the highest bidder? Is that it? If you wanted to sell yourself like that you should have just asked. I have plenty of money and I would have happily paid you for services rendered."

"Excuse me?" Her head swung up and he caught sight of the fire burning in her eyes. Uh oh. "Did you seriously just suggest I am your whore?"

"Not my words."

"But they'll do, right?" She stalked to the door and opened it. "You bastard. If you think anything I've done was for money then you don't know me at all. I do not need your money or anything else. Now I said get out and I meant it."

Tucker tamped the urge to keep going. He'd gone way past the point of no return. He glanced down at the jewelry box still sitting on her desk.

"What is that?" she asked.

"Nothing," he answered. "Nothing at all." Tucker grabbed his clothes and put them on without another word. He couldn't look at her for another second because it hurt too fucking much. His beautiful, sweet loving Maggie had betrayed him and the reality of that was more than he could bear. He walked through the door without looking at her again and slammed it shut behind him. Better to end it now before either one of them did anything more stupid.

Like confess.

CHAPTER FIFTEEN

Maggie stared at the closed door for a few seconds before she crumpled to the ground and let the tears fall at will. This wasn't at all what she'd expected. Confessions of love to accusations of betrayal all in one day. It made her head spin.

Why had she ever thought a memoir a good idea? Despite the brief bout of infamy with the media she doubted they cared enough to read a whole book. Her life simply wasn't that interesting. High school student to college student to college professor and wife. Her marriage may have been a sham but did anyone care but her? Unlikely.

She'd been a damn fool from the moment her life had exploded. Between thinking that a tell all book would shock the world to believing that Tucker was falling in love with her as much as she with him. As if people like them lived happily ever after.

More soaking wet tears tracked down her face. There was so much she didn't understand. In a way she'd lead a fairly sheltered life. Wonderful, if absentee parents who spent their lives giving to others gave her a solid relationship foundation to follow, yet her life had ended up nothing like theirs. She'd married out of a sense of duty to keep her career on the right track and a desire to finally get rid of her stupid virginity. It didn't help that she'd falsely convinced herself that she was in love with him. That fairy tale came to a screeching halt during the honeymoon when her brand new husband informed her their marriage had been one of convenience not love. Her virginity had stayed intact until the night she found her husband in bed with a man. The first of many to come.

He'd encouraged her to find someone to take care of her needs and she'd done precisely that. Twice. Maggie hated thinking about her ex. But there were no other men between him and Tucker that had meant anything to her. They'd merely scratched an itch.

She sighed and pushed herself off the floor. Lying in a pool of her tears wasn't going to get her past this. The best thing she could do was clean up and move on. Starting with the stupid book that wasn't ever going to happen in the first place. She moved to the desk to find and hit the delete key when she spied the box she'd seen Tucker holding. What the hell was it?

She picked it up and tried to calm her shaking stomach. She had a sinking feeling she wasn't going to like what she found inside. Steeling herself for the worst, she opened the lid and gasped. Nestled on the dark velvet sat a gorgeous silver chain-link necklace.

Was this—?

Then she saw the clasp. It was a small, handcrafted lock with a key sticking out of the end. *Oh. My. God.* Her hand flew to her mouth as fresh sobs tore from her throat and dissolved quickly into a torrent of uncontrollable tears that couldn't be stopped. She sat down on the chair and let them flow. For everything that had happened to her since she'd left her childhood behind to the grievous loss of Tucker in a blinding lack of trust. Everything she'd ever wanted had been decimated.

A long time passed before Maggie thought about moving. From her vantage point she noticed the sun shining bright outside. Where was the snow now when she preferred the gloom and doom to the golden glow of the sun?

What was she supposed to do now? When her world fell apart two months ago she'd immediately planned her retreat. She'd come back home, to gather her wits and do some writing until the media frenzy cooled. Every day that passed took her further away from her old life as she concentrated on her writing.

Then hurricane Tucker had struck and her world had turned upside down again. Had it only been a week? She found that hard to believe. When she left here she might leave with regrets but she would never forget her first Dom.

Maggie snorted. Who the hell was she kidding? Tucker owned her, always had. She'd find a new life and the past would again get buried in the back of her heart, but she would never ever forget. Even the harsh words he's flung at her in anger weren't enough to permanently burn off what she felt for him.

She glanced around her makeshift home. She didn't belong here. It was time to go. Putting one foot in front of the other she walked down the hall to the bedroom. Unable to look at the bed she'd shared with Tucker, she grabbed her clothes and headed into the bathroom. Somehow her brain tricked her into continuing as she blindly set about packing the house. Since Spring was still months away, she'd have to winterize everything, making sure to leave nothing behind.

If she left no trace of her visit maybe her parents wouldn't even realize she'd returned. At this point she'd do just about anything to avoid questions.

Maggie pulled boxes from the garage and hauled them in the house. She had half a plan to keep her brain occupied and push out thoughts of Tucker. Unfortunately, that didn't work. Everything she did, everything she touched, made her remember something about the man who'd given her a chance to be the woman she craved.

More tears burned behind her eyes. Maggie straightened her spine and drew in deep breaths. Regrets and alternative scenarios might fill her mind but that didn't mean she had to let them drag her into a deep pit of depression. It was her life and that meant it would be whatever she chose to make of it.

The phone rang after she started to pack, and her body froze. What if…

Nope. Don't even go there. Tucker wasn't going to magically call and tell her everything had been a huge mistake. It'd be a cold day in hell before she heard from him again.

By the third call in an hour she'd grown irritable and ready to take down the caller in a single phrase. Actually, she had several phrases in mind for the asshole on the other end. She stomped to her desk and grabbed the phone. "What?" she demanded.

"Is this Ms. Cisco? Maggie Cisco."

Her heart sank. For a second she'd still thought… maybe. "No comment," she blurted, assuming yet another reporter had found her.

"Pardon me?" The voice on the other end sounded very confused.

"Look, I know you're probably just doing your job but I'm in no mood for reporters today. This is a private number and I don't appreciate you calling it." As much as they deserved her wrath, the good manners bred in her still made it painful to be rude.

"Uhm. I'm not a reporter. My name is Carolyn Kellog and I'm calling on behalf of the University of Boston."

Maggie abruptly plopped into a nearby chair. "Seriously?"

The woman chuckled over the line. "Yes, seriously. We have a proposal for you. Would you have time to meet with us?"

Her head spun. "I don't understand. What is this about?" she held her breath, afraid to conjure any ideas in her mind.

"We have a job we'd like you to consider. But we'd rather discuss it in person. If you're free we'd like to fly you in to meet with us."

Her breath left her body in a whoosh. A job? She hadn't considered going back to teaching even a possibility. Nor was she sure she wanted to. Not that she had a lot of choices at the moment. She'd yet to come up with a single idea of where she'd go. With no family to flee to and no friends not tied into her old life, she'd have to go somewhere new. Maybe...

"When would you like me to come?"

"Are you available tomorrow?"

"Tomorrow sounds perfect." After listening to the travel details that would be emailed to her, Maggie hung up and surveyed the room. Packing the cabin could wait. She had a plane to catch.

*

Forty-eight hours later Maggie walked into Nina's café at the edge of the lake. Since she hadn't bothered to stop for any supplies after her plane landed, she stopped at the only place she could to get some food to take home with her.

Home.

Not for long. She had a week to get things packed up and moved to Boston. The sadness never far from her conscious came rushing forward. Her step faltered. The nonstop ache for Tucker seized her insides. No matter how hard she tried to get him out of her head, he'd taken up residence and no amount of busy work kept him at bay.

Less than twenty-four hours away from him and she'd sat down at her computer to send him an email. Shame at being unable to resist him still burned inside her. Still, whether or not he hated her she'd made sure he understood there would never be a book. Her attempt to get back to writing through a journal had been a colossal error on her part. At the very least, her conscience was clear.

Coming here had been a mistake. She didn't want to make small talk with Tucker's sister and pretend that everything was fine. Or worse suffer Nina's wrath for her perceived betrayal. Maggie sighed. Either way, she'd be tempted to ask about him and finding out he'd already moved on after a mere two days would likely kill her. Not that she had much room to talk. Twenty minutes after her interview at University of Boston, she'd made the decision to move north.

If only to escape.

The idea of running into Tucker, or driving past the turn off to his estate every day knowing she no longer belonged there made her stomach twist into knots and acid churn within. So Boston it would be. Although she'd had no luck finding an apartment for rent on such short notice. She figured a little time in front of her computer would solve that problem. That's what realtors and Craigslist were for.

The too familiar burn of oncoming tears made the decision to leave without dinner an easy one. No way in hell did she want to face Nina yet. Maggie turned around and headed back out the door.

"Excuse me. Where do you think you're going young lady?"

Maggie froze at the strong sound of Nina's voice. Slowly she turned and faced the woman. "I—uh—"

"Yeah, you uh-uh, whatever. Get your ass back in here and grab a table. You look like you could use a strong cup of coffee and some food."

Maggie had no idea what to say to that so she obediently followed Nina back into the café. Somehow she'd get through this without asking about Tucker. She had to. She was better off not knowing.

"Take the booth in the corner and I'll be right back with your coffee. I've got two customers to take care of and then it's just you and me." Nina rushed off before Maggie could respond.

She slid into the booth and pushed her purse to her side. She inhaled deeply. Something in the diner smelled so damned good it made her mouth water. Maggie pressed a hand to her stomach to halt the rumbling. Had she stopped to eat anything since she'd left her hotel room that morning? She couldn't remember. Some of the fatigue from her whirlwind two days began to catch up with her as she sank bonelessly into the supple leather seat of the booth. She rested her head on the cushion behind her and closed her eyes.

A busy couple of days wasn't her problem at all. She missed Tucker. For the first time in her life, she'd really felt like she belonged. Not as a doted on child, or an ornament on someone's arm, but a real participant. That sensation had left her thoughts about research scattered as she tried to transition from observer to participant to researcher again.

Her body began to release some of its tension as warmth seeped into her bones. Boston in the wintertime had proven harsh and she wasn't used to that. When the plane landed back in North Carolina, she'd breathed a momentary sigh of relief to see the gorgeous Carolina blue sky.

"Wake up sleeping beauty. You need some nourishment before you pass out."

Maggie cracked an eye open to discover Nina hovering at the edge of the table with a mug of coffee and a bowl of some delicious-smelling soup. "Thank you."

"Don't thank me yet." Nina slid into the booth across from her. "I plan to grill you about my brother."

Maggie groaned. "Do you have to?"

"Of course I do. What are sisters for if not to butt into her brother's life? Besides, I care about what happens to you to. And from my vantage point I'm guessing you're both acting like a couple of asses."

Maggie took a bite of the smoky corn chowder and gave herself a second to regroup. "Anyone ever tell you that you have a succinct way of putting things?"

Nina shrugged. "Just because you uptight types aren't used to someone telling it like it is, doesn't mean I'm letting you or Tucker off the hook. Now spill. Tell me why my brother is not answering my calls or his front door."

Maggie winced and averted her eyes. Had their break up had that much of an effect on him? Surely not. "You're probably overreacting. We both know he's prone to fall off the grid when he's in his studio."

"Don't even try to bullshit a bullshitter. Tucker came by here on Sunday morning before he went to Mayfield and wouldn't shut up about you. Now he's gone silent? No one turns around that quickly over some art. Not even my brother. Besides, it's too damned cold for him to work the glass. He won't be back at it full time until Spring comes round. Oops. There went your final excuse."

What the hell, Nina was going to find out sooner or later. If Tucker wouldn't listen to her, maybe getting the truth off her chest to Nina would make it easier to leave.

"Tucker thinks I was planning to betray his trust to the media by writing a book that included details about his sexual life," she blurted.

Nina cocked an eye. "Oh boy. And are you?"

"Of course not! I've never written about someone who hadn't given me their express permission beforehand. Of course, the horse's ass would have known that if he'd given me five minutes to explain before making his assumptions."

Her friend laughed. "I take it you're not happy with him right now."

"Happy? Does this haggard, bags-under-my-eyes face look happy to you?"

"So what are you going to do about it?"

"I'm going to pick up the pieces and move on. I've received a new job offer in Boston and I plan to take it. I have a few days to pack and then I'll be out of Tucker's life for good." Putting the thoughts to words tore through her chest.

Nina leaned in close. "You should see your face. Maybe you were able to say you were leaving but your expression said it all. You don't want to leave anymore than I imagine my boneheaded brother wants you to."

Maggie straightened her back and set down her spoon. No way could she eat now. "You're wrong. His words to me couldn't have been anymore final if he'd driven me to the airport himself."

"It's true, he's stubborn as a pack mule, I'll give you that. But you're the first woman I've ever seen him serious about." She held up her hand. "No wait, before you protest. I know he dropped you off at home on Sunday morning. Did he tell you where he was going? Where he goes every single Sunday year after year after year."

She shook her head. She'd been so wrapped up in the afterglow of their scenes she'd thought very little of anything else that weekend.

"That's what I thought. Well, since he's too close-mouthed to talk about it then I will. I'll take the heat from him later, but I think it will be worth it." She glanced around. "I know you're familiar with our father. I mean who wouldn't be. Before his death he'd risen to a pretty powerful figure around here. With his religious convictions and presumably endless devotion to family, he traded on that power for a lot of wealth. He built an empire that to this day remains strong and unbreakable."

"I don't understand. What does this have to do with where he went on Sunday. Your father passed away years ago."

"Thank God."

Maggie sat back, shocked by Nina's exclamation.

"I know. I know. You don't understand. No one does and that's the way Tucker wants to keep it. The less the public knows the better." Nina covered Maggie's hands. "The point I'm trying to get to is this. Just before his death, something really bad happened. No. I can't tell you but you can trust me that it's pretty bad and his mom had a full mental breakdown. A catatonic, no longer speaks kind of breakdown, and she's never recovered."

"What—?"

"No. That's all you're getting out of me. You need to talk to Tucker. He's the one who needs to open up with you before he can really trust. Until then you'll both be stuck. Him going out to the sanitarium to see his mother every weekend as the focus of his life and you never understanding why he is the way he is." Nina stood. "Talk to him. Bang down his door if you have to. If you can get the truth out of him then I'll know I was right all along."

"Right about what?" Maggie asked, but Nina had already walked off and was speaking to a customer at another table.

CHAPTER SIXTEEN

Maggie checked the clock on her dash for the umpteenth time. Like it or not her time was up. It had been two days since her chat with Nina and the silence since deafened her. She checked her phone too frequently for word from Tucker to no avail. The man had written her off.

The bone-deep sadness that thought created burned inside her. Despite Nina's solemn wisdom and information about some of what held Tucker back, Maggie couldn't bring herself to go see him. She couldn't take seeing the despair and belief in her betrayal across his face again. It was enough she spent half her night in bed reliving that last day with him. Loneliness weighed on her.

She pulled up to the cabin and rushed to the front door. The weather report called for more snow tonight and she wanted to be inside by a cozy fire long before the first flake fell. She unlocked the door, and stepped inside her warm house and froze in place, her feet rooted to the ground.

Standing larger than life in front her was a giant portrait of her on Tucker's bondage wheel. It took her a full thirty seconds before she could breathe and another thirty for her to move. Her gaze bounced around the room, seeking Tucker, to only find the room empty. Her heart squeezed. For a split second she'd thought...

Maggie moved closer to the portrait and studied it. He'd captured the stark sensuality of their scene exactly as she remembered it. Her facial expression managed to convey intense lust with a hint of fear. His art skills were amazing. Not a detail had been missed. It didn't take much to be transported back to that first day as she stood there watching him draw. Her body quivered at the memory. She'd interviewed submissives who talked a lot about how hard their Doms made them come. That day she'd learned exactly what that meant. With his attention everywhere on her body she'd experienced firsthand that mind blowing, mind altering orgasms were hard to forget.

What did it mean that he'd brought this here? Did he want to see her again? Or was he simply removing all trace of her from his life?

Maggie sighed. Would the physical and mental ache for her Master ever go away?

Too tired to make dinner or do more than change her clothes, Maggie left the painting behind and went to bed. Tomorrow her new life would start and this one would end forever.

Unfortunately, after hours of tossing and turning, sleep continued to elude her. She grabbed her pillow and a blanket and returned to the living room. Here the faint scent of Tucker's playroom filled her senses and made it easier to relax. She had to stop thinking like this. The longer she allowed him to dominate her thoughts the longer it would take for her to move on.

She eased onto the pillow and snuggled under the blanket. Tomorrow for certain she'd let it go. Maggie wondered if Tucker missed her as much as she missed him. He'd been planning to give her—

Maggie bolted upright. The collar! Oh crap. She'd forgotten all about it. She had to get it back to him. Her gaze shot to the clock above the couch. Only 9:30. Still early enough. She slumped. What if he didn't want to see her? Nina's assurance that Tucker deserved a second chance pushed at her brain.

It's now or never, idiot.

Before she could talk herself out of it, she got dressed, grabbed the jewelry box from her desk and headed out the door.

* * *

When the doorbell rang and Tucker checked the security camera a sense of Déjà vu overcame him. She'd come.

He opened the front door and had a small box

thrust in his face.

"Here, I wanted to make sure I got this back to you before I left."

She stood before him dressed in form-fitting pants that hugged the curves of her legs with a parka zipped up to her chin and the hood pulled over her hair. Her eyes were wide and she refused to look at him directly.

One glance at her and the tumble of emotions he'd been fighting for the last several days overtook him. Guilt, anger, love… They were all there and driving him insane. He'd spent the first two days obsessed with her painting, making small subtle changes that brought her to life on canvas. That had only made things worse.

"Take it, Tucker. I don't know what else to do with it." The soft plead in her voice unraveled the last of his reservations. How she conveyed so much sorrow in a few words he'd never know.

"I don't want the damn necklace. I want the sub that comes with it." He growled the words, making them sound far harsher than he'd intended.

Her hand dropped to her side and tears shimmered in her eyes, the look on her face breaking his heart in two. Tucker grabbed her jacket and pulled her to him. He had to make her forget the vile shit that had come from his mouth. She deserved so much better. If she ever decided to write a book so be it. He'd have Mason buy the fucking publishing house and make sure it never saw the light of day.

"I'm sorry." Two words were all he could get out before he had to kiss her. He wound his hand behind her head and jacket, tugged her close and crushed his mouth against hers. He poured everything he felt into the one kiss. He couldn't help it. His world had gone dark the moment he'd walked away from her, making it damned difficult to think or act straight.

Heated lust flooded through him. He'd already gone hard the minute he opened the door and now his erection pressing against her soft body made his head spin. With need riding him harder than the devil at a church revival, he dragged her into the house and against the wall.

His head screamed conquer while his tongue delved into the sweet heat of his Maggie.

Mine. The word repeated in his head on an endless loop.

First, he had to get this jacket off of her. He wanted her skin touching his. Without tearing from her mouth, his fingers made quick work of getting the infernal puffy jacket that hid her from him, off her body. To his surprise she pushed against him, squashing her breasts into his chest. *Can't breathe*.

He tore from her mouth and gulped for air. Besides the lack of oxygen, it felt like all the blood in his body had rushed to his groin. "Need. Oh God, Maggie. Baby." He stroked her face. "I really fucked up, but I need you so bad I can barely breathe. I have to have you."

Her lips parted and her eyes widened, zeroing in on him. This time he had her full attention. "You've had me from the beginning."

That simple confession broke him. He reached for the thin shirt she'd worn under her jacket and ripped it down the front. He pushed her bra over her tits and buried his face between them. Her familiar sweet scent flooded his senses. *Oh fuck yes.*

"I can't be gentle," he warned.

Her small fingers threaded through his hair and held him tight. "Don't care about gentle," she panted.

He groaned into her soft flesh. He was pretty sure she'd just melted his brain. There was no way in hell he deserved this woman with her beautiful trusting eyes watching his every move. Not that anything could stop him now. He loved her. He nibbled a path from her breasts to her neck, placing a series of kisses across her sweet skin.

He wanted to slow things down and savor her but his body had a mind of its own. His fingers yanked at her pants until they were halfway down her legs. He got to his knees and helped her step out of them before he flung them aside. With their bodies perfectly positioned he leaned forward and pressed a kiss to her mound. When his fingers slid between the lips of her pussy his eyes rolled to the back of his head she felt so fucking good. "You're so wet for me." He easily slipped a finger inside her and fucked her with it.

With his free hand, he jerked at the button and zipper of his pants until his cock sprang free. Being released from confinement gave him little relief. His whole body throbbed to be inside her. Fucking her until they'd both learned their lesson about separation.

"We can't do this again. Do you hear me, Maggie? Never."

She nodded her head, tears falling down her cheeks. She cried out when he removed his hand from her pussy. He pinched a nipple to distract her. "Hold onto my neck and wrap your legs around me." He scooped her into his arms and she quickly complied, leaving his cock perfectly aligned with the entrance to her cunt.

Without pause, he tunneled his way inside, sinking all the way to the hilt in one smooth continuous move. Her cry made him hesitate there as her body quickly adjusted to him. He pushed her back against the wall and withdrew to the tip. She gasped and tightened her hold around his neck and waist.

"Don't worry baby, I'm not going anywhere." He pressed in and pulled out with more force than usual. It couldn't be helped. His control was shot. He'd make it up to her later. Hell, there were an endless stream of ideas for what he could do to his sub constantly running through his head. She had no idea how much trouble she was in.

He slammed harder, making sure each thrust hit the spot she needed. He craned his neck to watch her beautiful face flush as she came apart in his arms. Never in a million years would he get tired of watching her come. The muscles of her pussy contracted around him and he realized she was dragging him with her. Damn, he loved her. He buried his face in her neck and groaned through the short, quivering digs of his release. Still, he couldn't stop. The Neanderthal inside him wanted to ensure his claim would never be forgotten. Before long, common sense grabbed a hold of him and he slumped against her, using his weight to support them both.

"Mine, Maggie. Mine."

Her body jerked and the next thing he knew her small fists were pummeling his chest. "You can't say that to me. It's not right," she cried.

Afraid he'd hurt her in this position, he withdrew from her body and carried her to the sofa.

"Put me down this instant," she demanded.

Tucker arched his brow and considered doing a whole lot more than putting her down. Except they needed to talk, so he released her and she scrambled off the couch and grabbed her clothes.

"Don't," he warned. They definitely weren't finished.

"Don't *don't* me. It's ridiculous, this is ridiculous." She waved her arms back and forth around them. "You can't tell me this can never happen again and then call me yours. It's cruel." Some of the fight left her body as tears streamed down her cheeks and she buried her face in her hands. She broke his heart.

"What are you talking about? That's not what I meant. Fuck." He fisted his fingers into his hair and collapsed onto the couch. "I can't live without you."

Her head jerked up. "What?"

He wanted to cross to her and scoop her into his arms but he knew where that led. This time they had to talk so he stayed in his seat.

"I'm an ass, Maggie. At the first sign of trouble I assumed you had lied to me. I wish I could take it all back but I can't. I was cruel and harsh and everything I've always feared." He held his breath for a few seconds. She'd never forgive him unless he told her the truth.

"Trust is really hard for me. Hell, a lot of emotion is hard for me."

She stepped closer. "That's now how I saw you."

He grimaced. "Saw being the operative word here. Until my paranoia got the better of me and I ruined everything."

She took another step. "No, don't touch me right now. I'm like a live wire and won't hesitate to have you under me again. We have to finish this. I have to get this out or I never will."

"You probably don't remember much about my father other than what he allowed the public to see.

He came off to everyone around him as a righteous religious man with hard-core beliefs. Hell, even I bought into that. He rode my ass every day of my life until I left for college and even then he had no problem checking up on me at every opportunity. He nagged me to death and I hated him for it."

Tucker squeezed his eyes shut and tried to block out the image of his father's last night. There were some things too painful to discuss. He pushed the memories out of his mind and went back to the easier part of the story.

"One Friday night while in college, I decided to come home for the weekend. I loaded a few of my friends into my car and we showed up here unannounced. The minute we walked through the door, the world went to shit. A young woman was here. She'd gotten stinking drunk and chosen that night to come to the house to confront my asshole father."

Despite trying to implement every coping mechanism he'd ever learned, much of the rage from that night bled through. "She wanted my mother to know what kind of man she'd married."

"I thought your mom already knew he'd had an affair?

"Oh she did and that's why she left him for a while. Until he found her and convinced her that he'd confessed his sins to God and prayed for forgiveness. My mother had always been devout in her religion and she forgave him. Of course he'd lied through his teeth. What he'd managed to keep from us all was far worse. There wasn't only one. Apparently, my father's religious beliefs were more extreme than anyone knew. He'd married and impregnated over a dozen women during his marriage to my mom. There were children everywhere."

Maggie covered her mouth and smothered a small gasp.

"Still not the worst part." The rest of the story felt like a giant lump in his throat. He'd spent nearly a decade trying to forget. "The woman who confronted him that night was one of his children. On her eighteenth birthday he tried to…"

"No! Oh God, Tucker don't. You don't have to say it." She ran into his arms and wrapped herself around him.

Numb now, he rambled on. "Do you remember when my dad was hospitalized from a hunting accident?"

Maggie nodded.

"Not a hunting accident. That poor girl's mother shot him."

"Tucker, I don't know what to say. I had no idea."

"Don't. There's nothing you need to say. What I wanted you to understand is how fucked up I've been. My mom hasn't spoken a word since that day and it breaks my heart every week when I visit her. But I can't stop going to see her. And my dad…

Well, he was a sex addicted serial cheater who used some whacked out religious beliefs as an excuse to impregnate half the county and I carry his fucking DNA. Do you understand what that means? Whatever short circuited in his logical thought processes could happen again. I could end up like him."

"Bullshit!" she exclaimed. "I don't believe that for a second."

The fierce look of belief on her face took his breath away. It made him sick how little trust he'd shown her previously. "I believe that now. But when I was twenty-one years old, my friends and I had already started Purgatory. We spent our spare time whipping women. In the face of the asshole's revelations it seemed pretty fucked up. So we withdrew. We wanted to sell the club and cut our ties from the past, but my father's will made a normal life impossible. He'd left a fortune behind. A fortune I might add that was built on the backs of this small town and everyone in it. He split everything equally among all his living children with a lot of codicils and conditions."

"That sounds complicated."

"Exactly. Being able to keep the money depends on keeping his secrets. All of them. Of course, the first thing I wanted to do was tell them all to go to hell. The lawyers, the financial managers, everyone. As far as I was concerned every last dime could rot in the ground with him."

She touched his cheek with her warm fingers. "Family matters are never without complications and obligations are they?"

"Never," he answered honestly. "Fortunately, my friend Mason was here for me back then. When I couldn't cope with it anymore than my mom could, he took over. There were babies involved. Fuck, there are so many people wrapped up in my father's lies it takes a small army to keep it contained. We've done a pretty decent job over the years."

"And then you met me."

He slapped her bottom. "Not what I meant at all. More like your return has woken me up and I want something more than just getting by. Things have to change."

"But I come with too much baggage. If privacy is what you need to keep everyone taken care of, I can't promise that. If I stay here there's a somewhat decent chance a news truck will eventually roll in and disrupt our lives. We can never work." The finality in her voice tore through him, wrapped around his chest.

"You're not getting away from me that easy. You poked the bear and now you're stuck with him."

She frowned up at him. "Hardly. More like the bear hunted me down and threatened to eat me if I didn't do what he said."

Tucker laughed and Maggie smiled, transforming her sadness in a heart beat. "You're so beautiful when you smile. I think I'll have to find new ways every day to make you do that." He kissed her mouth, only lingering for a few extra seconds. "I love you, Maggie."

"Oh God. Tucker." Her smile vanished and tears shimmered in her eyes. "As much as I love you, I don't see how we can work."

"One day at a time." He kissed her again, this time delving into her warm mouth. He'd drag her to his dark side using kisses and more if he had to. With more than a little reluctance, he released her mouth. "Mason and I will find a way to control the situation. We always do. What matters the most is that we can trust you and if you can live with who I am and where I come from, I'd really like to keep you."

"Which you? The hardheaded man who jumps to conclusions or the Dom who has the power to bring me to my knees and love every second of it?"

He grinned at her assessment of him. "That's the whole package, Miss Maggie. Although I hope you'll find it in your heart to forget and forgive the conclusion jumping. I was an ass, but I'd like to think I learn from my mistakes."

"Are you ever going to quit calling me Miss Maggie?"

"Nope. Calling you Miss Maggie reminds me that you've been the one for me since that first kiss. I'm never letting that go."

Her mouth dropped open. "You don't really

believe that do you? Since the first kiss?"

Tucker shrugged. "You marked me that night. We might not have realized it then, but that's what happened. No kiss since then has been as memorable."

She wiggled in his lap, rubbing her bottom across his crotch. "No kiss?"

He tightened his grip on her arms. "Careful, Maggie. Acting like a brat will get you more than you bargained for. I've already settled on how the rest of this night will go. So give me a kiss and then go in the bedroom and wait for me."

The change in her demeanor from his words alarmed him. She went from warm and happy to tense and awkward in a few seconds.

"I can't. Oh shit I forgot." She scrambled from his lap and reached for her tattered clothes. "I have to go home, I have an early morning flight."

"Maggie, stop. What the hell are you talking about? Flight? Where are you going?"

She slowly turned in his direction. "I accepted a new job in Boston. I leave tomorrow."

CHAPTER SEVENTEEN

"You did what?" He couldn't believe what he was hearing. "In just a few short days you not only found a new job, but you're leaving tomorrow?"

"What was I supposed to do? Mope and eat bon bons? Maybe spend a month watching Lifetime sap? That's not who I am. I might have cried while I did it, but I was determined to give you what you wanted and get as far away as possible."

"That's not at all what I want, baby." She couldn't leave now.

"Well, I know that now. Unfortunately I have a new commitment and I have to leave tomorrow."

He stood from the couch and crossed the room. He grabbed the clothes from her hands and threw them in the corner. "You can find a job here if you want."

She placed her hands on her hips and pushed out her breasts. "Not like this one I can't and I'll thank you to quit manhandling my clothes already. Relax, I'll only be gone six weeks. The college in Boston offered me a chance to be a guest lecturer for a special class they are sponsoring."

He rubbed his temples, hoping to stop the spinning. She was damned hard to keep up with. "A class? I thought your heart wasn't really in teaching anymore. If you still want to teach, we've got a great college here in town."

She laughed and shook her head. "Right. Because the Christian college is dying to hire an instructor who specializes in alternative lifestyles. No thank you. The University of Boston is starting a series of classes on sexuality in today's modern media and the first class is about the runaway bestseller of erotic fiction that has seemingly turned the world upside down."

He closed and opened his eyes and examined the room. Nope still spinning. "This is for real?"

"I know! It's all a bit surreal. As it turns out I'll be using the book as a case study to discuss its impact on the American culture and sexual health in general. It's an opportunity too good to pass up."

She continued to describe her interview and the direction she wanted to take the class in. The passion she exuded excited him. There was a fire burning in her about this and no man had the right to squelch that. "I'll go with you then," he blurted

It took a few seconds before his statement sunk in. Her words trailed off and her eyes grew wide. "You'd do that for me?"

He grabbed her by the waist and pulled her against him. "It's the least I can do for you. It will give me lots of time to make things up to you." He slid his hands into her hair, gripped the short strands and pulled her head back. "Now come to bed with me and let me love you like you deserve. There are still many hours until tomorrow morning."

"Oh, Tucker…"

* * *

Tucker stood at the end of the bed and let his gaze roam over the woman splayed on her stomach across the mattress. The sweet contour of her neck and spine was almost as beautiful as the full round curve of her gorgeous ass. He'd thought about taking her there since they'd reunited, he'd even threatened it more than once.

He walked forward with the tools he'd retrieved from his studio. Fortunately for him, her arms were already spread out and in the perfect position. It took him only a few minutes to tie each wrist to one of the eyehooks attached to his bed.

He set the various paint brushes he'd brought to the room on the bed and chose the largest and softest one of them all. With a feather light touch, he brushed her porcelain perfect skin from shoulder to hip. "Time to wake up, my submissive."

"Ohhh…" she moaned.

He continued his path across her lower back and dipped into the swell of her ass checks. To his delight, she began to squirm. Wouldn't take long now for her to realize his intentions. He felt a smile tug at his lips. She looked particularly gorgeous spread out before him. He imagined enjoying this position quite a lot.

Tucker continued to paint her skin sans paint. It didn't take much imagination to envision the vivid colors swirling across her skin. She definitely inspired him. If it were up to him he'd paint her over and over in every position imaginable. He'd fill their home with her sensual image.

Which reminded him that this wasn't the house he imagined them beginning their life in. The property held so much bad luck and bad memories. They both deserved a fresh start. If she agreed, the first thing they'd do when they returned from Boston was house hunt.

He ran his paintbrush further between her cheeks and traveled the bottom curve of each buttock before traveling down one of her legs. She stirred hard and her arms jerked against the restraints.

"What the hell?"

He chuckled. "I told you this would happen. Did you forget?" He was her Dom and living up to things he promised was more important than ever. They were rebuilding the trust damaged the last few days. "Maybe you thought I was joking when I said I'd wake you up tied down with my dick in your ass." He slid the blunt end of the brush between her cheeks and prodded the tiny opening that awaited him. "We're about to get to the second part."

She gasped. "You're serious?"

"About that? Always."

Maggie shuddered, her legs opening a fraction more. "There isn't time? I have a flight…"

"Stop worrying. This is about you and the pleasure I need to give you."

"But the flight," she half whined and half moaned.

He smacked her ass with the wooden handle of his brush, the loud thwap music to his ears.

Maggie let out a breathy cry but didn't protest again. Tucker grabbed her leg and spread it wider so he could fasten her ankle to the bedpost with another silk tie.

"There's no need to even think about trying to catch a flight. We've got a private plane at our disposal, so we can leave whenever we're ready." He picked up her second foot, fastened it in place and stood back to admire the beauty of his submissive tied and ready.

"You have a plane?" she panted her question.

He loved that sound. The edge of arousal when Maggie barely breathed and a slight tremor ran through her arms and legs. He made a mental note to make that his new daily goal.

"*We* have a plane, little one. What I have is yours *and* mine. Now stop talking about planes and keep quiet. The only sound I want to hear is your scream of pleasure or if you need it, your safe word. Is that understood?"

"Yes, Master."

Tucker sighed, that new found sense of satisfaction filling him again. Not to mention, with the sun streaming in through the windows, he had a perfect vantage point with incredible lighting. Her body made him want to do very wicked things to her. He felt a smile crawl across his face as he once again trailed the soft bristles of the brush down her leg to the bottom of one foot.

She flinched at the light touch, her leg jerking hard against the silk restraint. "Oh—God—Tucker that tickles."

He tested her toes to the same result as well as her ankles. Damn, she was too fun to play with. Every inch of her proved to be as sexy and sweet as the rest. Around and around he swirled until her body shuddered uncontrollably. He flung the soft brush to the side and picked up the small, stiff one that would create a totally different sensation.

He took a moment to check on her wrists and ankles to ensure they weren't too constricting and gave her a break with the soft touch of his hands on the backs of her thighs. Tucker allowed his fingers to travel higher to the heat between her legs. Her wetness allowed him to slide straight into her opening with no barrier. Her body shook so hard he half expected her to come long before he sank into her asshole.

He purposely avoided touching her clit. He doubted it would take much for her at the moment. With his fingers buried in her pussy, rubbing against the sensitive inner walls, he scraped his second brush sharply across her bottom several times. Many of the bristles were clumped together from old paint and were no longer soft. They left pretty red streaks behind on her ass.

He rewarded her cry by shoving his fingers deeper, making sure to rub the one spot almost guaranteed to send her flying. She bucked her hips and lifted her ass as much as her restraints allowed. Satisfied that she'd been properly aroused, he pulled his hand away and lifted his fingers to his mouth. He made sure to suckle them loudly so she'd know exactly what he'd done. "I love your taste, little sub. So tangy. Mmm." He licked them clean. "If I didn't already have my heart set on getting inside you right now, I'd be buried between your legs making you come so hard you'd flood my mouth."

His little sub cried out. It was so much fun to find out what things he did and said turned her on and dirty talk got her hot. "Like that huh?"

He turned and reached for the rest of his supplies. "Then you're going to love these." He held up the two gold balls connected by wire to a remote control that he'd ordered just for her.

Maggie turned her head and when her gaze focused on them her eyes glazed and she groaned.

"You're going to kill me."

Anxious to get the show on the road, Tucker climbed on the bed between her legs. The faint red lines on her ass and the glistening cream on the lips of her pussy were like a glaring *come and get me* sign. He wasted no time working the egg-sized balls inside her. "Ready, Maggie?"

"Yes, Master."

He picked up the small remote and turned the power to low.

"Ohhh," she moaned. A sound he really enjoyed.

Next he grabbed for the tube of lube and squirted it on to her small anal pucker. She shook her head back and forth and wiggled against his hand, but maintained her silence. So far so good.

"Don't worry, baby. I'm going to warm you up a little with my fingers first. I want you to enjoy it, not be afraid of it." With more lube slathered on his fingers, he pressed one to her opening and slowly eased inside. "That's it, little one, relax and let me do the work."

"What if I need to come? Am I allowed?"

He pushed his finger to the hilt and stilled. "If you get to the point you can't wait, then yes, you may come. But don't think I'll stop or slow down. I'll simply drive you to another one." He grit his teeth against the building need to simply plow into her. She needed finesse on his part and damned if he wouldn't give it to her. He was crouched close enough he could feel the heat coming from her cunt and her ass was doing its level best to strangle his finger. He could only imagine what she'd do to his dick when he got inside her.

With as much patience as he could muster, he pulled his finger to the edge of her opening and added a second finger before he pushed back inside. She tensed for a moment and he had to stop and wait for her to relax again. He ran his free hand over the back of her thighs until he found the remote waiting for him by her knee. He flipped the switch to medium and waited for the extra sensations to distract her.

It didn't take long before her body began to shake and he easily fucked his fingers in and out of her ass. It amazed him that Maggie hadn't been snapped up by a Dom long before now. Her husband hadn't deserved her and he probably didn't either, but he wasn't letting go now. She belonged to him and his intention was to enjoy every day for the pleasure he gave her.

Her moans and cries grew louder, signaling her oncoming orgasm. Tucker removed his fingers and switched off the remote. He expected a protest but none came. Instead, she wiggled and rubbed, lost in the exquisite sensations.

He quickly unrolled the condom he'd added to his toys and added more lube to his cock. He eased into position behind her and pressed the tip of his flesh to her primed and ready opening. "Tell me you want this, Maggie."

She murmured something into the sheets he couldn't make out. His little sub was too far gone. He began to push inside and hesitated. At the last second he turned the vibrating balls back on and gently tunneled inside as she shuddered underneath him.

"Master!" she screamed as the vibrations and probably the edge of pain from his cock, sent her careening into release. Tucker's eyes nearly rolled back in his head at the incredible sensation of her little muscles clenching around him over and over. So damned good. He moaned.

Heat sizzled from his cock to his head. He grabbed her buttocks and held her tight as he pushed as far as he could go. His balls drew up tight, his arms shook. They were both on total overload.

"Oh Tucker, please. Don't stop."

Her exclamation broke something inside him. Emotion swelled and overwhelmed him. His sub. His woman. His love.

She fought underneath him, straining for something as a constant stream of pleading for more met his ears. He'd driven her to the brink of lust and now she demanded to be sated and he was more than happy to oblige.

The words easy and soft fled from his mind as he began fucking her as wildly as she cried. He pulled back and shoved in, her tight channel gripping him tighter than before. The combination of him filling her and the balls vibrating must have been too much. Maggie's short screams changed to a long, loud wail as she came. The exquisite sound wrapped around Tucker and embraced his soul. He couldn't move as fire sizzled through his blood and Maggie thrashed against him, milking his release from him. The pure perfection of the woman beneath him took his breath away. He'd finally found where he belonged.

Tucker fell against her, barely able to hold himself up. He fought to catch his breath as he eased off her as gently as he could. At the end they'd both lost control and he'd been rough. He worried he'd hurt her.

He trailed a line of kisses along her spine as he moved from the bed. Despite his still-shaking limbs, he untied her ankles and wrists, taking care to massage each one and then disappeared into the bathroom. In slow motion, he disposed of the condom and grabbed a wet cloth and a dry one. A glance in the mirror shocked him. He appeared wild eyed and savage. Afraid to analyze what he saw, he rushed back into the bedroom and began his care of Maggie.

She smelled so good. The scent of sex and Maggie went together extremely well. Before he got distracted from his good intentions, he dragged his thoughts back to her care. "I'd like to put you into a nice warm bath, little one. We've got time."

She mumbled sleepily and then smiled at him.

"Are you okay, Maggie?"

One eye opened. "Oh hell, I'm way more than all right. I'm in love with my Master," she crooned.

His heart clenched. He dropped the towels and climbed back into bed with her. A bath could wait. "I love you, my sub." He placed a kiss on her shoulder. "More than I ever thought possible."

There was one more thing he'd brought into the bedroom this morning and she wasn't leaving without it. He reached for the delicate silver collar she'd nearly shoved in his face last night.

"Maggie, roll over." She grumbled something about him being mean before she complied. She was so incredible. He loved the vinegar as much as the sugar in this woman. She fit in here better than she thought she did. She'd learn though. Once the women of Davidson got it through their thick skulls that she'd taken him off the market, she'd get along fine.

"Why do you look so serious?" She reached up and rubbed his forehead where he'd probably been scrunching his face as she'd so lovingly put it before.

"Because I have something serious to give you." He placed the tip of the bare chain on her gently rounded belly and dragged it up to the hollow of her neck. His heart pounded in his chest at the prospect of collaring Maggie permanently. To him it was as important as getting married.

"I don't know if you understand how much this

means to me, but I want to put this collar on your neck and lock it. Only I'll have the key because you're mine. Mine to love. Mine to fuck when I want. And mine to pleasure for the rest of your life."

A small tear escaped the corner of her eye and Tucker leaned down to lick it clean. Even her tears belonged to him.

"Oh Tucker." He placed a finger across her lips so he could continue.

"You wearing it is an intense personal commitment for us, but it's also a symbol to others that you're committed to your Dom. If you'll have me of course."

She moved to sit up and then cupped his cheek. "I'd be honored to wear your collar."

"I had this made as a cross between an old fashioned collar and a traditional necklace. Anyone in the lifestyle will likely recognize it, while others won't think twice about it. Although considering your current reputation, it might garner some notice." He used the key to undo the lock and slipped the collar around her neck. The two ends were pulled together and he slid the lock between the two connecting rings. Before he clicked it shut, he stared down at her. "Are you sure?"

"Without a doubt."

The tiny lock snicked closed and settled at the hollow of her throat. Tucker pulled Maggie into his arms.

"So this is really happening? You're really going

to Boston with me? I'm not going to wake up from a dream or anything, right?"

He pinched her arm.

"Owww!" she cried. "Why'd you do that?"

He didn't even try to hide his smile. "Nope, definitely not a dream. But if you'd like to be sure, I've got a spanking bench in the playroom with your name written all over it, Miss Maggie."

EPILOGUE

Tucker took a seat across from Mason in one of the smooth leather booths in the back room of the restaurant. They'd agreed to meet here because it afforded both of them a decent amount of privacy. At this early hour not too many Doms had made their way to this area. He glanced across the space to the table he'd occupied with Maggie only a couple of weeks ago. Felt like a lifetime now. So much had changed and happened since then.

"I see you managed to break away from the ball and chain."

Tucker flipped him off. "Whatever. You're just jealous you don't have a sub right now."

His friend simply lifted his shoulders. Mason looked tired. The years of secrets and separation had taken their toll on all of them, but Mason seemed the most affected. He guessed it was easy to say that now that he had Maggie. He'd never felt freer in his life. Except when he remembered all she didn't yet know.

"I need to tell her everything." Might as well

blurt it out and get this party started.

"Some secrets aren't yours to tell." The pained look in Mason's eyes let Tucker know he referred to Nina. When it came to her Mason was worse than a mother bear. He'd protect her at all costs and God forbid if anyone got in his way.

"I'm going to ask her to marry me as soon as we return from Boston. I can't start a marriage with lies and you know that."

His friend shrugged. "You already did, my friend. Marriage is merely a legal device and we both know the collar you put around her neck is far more meaningful. You waited all your life for her."

He did indeed. Funny how life worked out sometimes. Of course Mason was right. He may have bound Maggie to him as his submissive, but when she found out he'd kept most of the truth from her, she might still run.

"We can trust her, Mace."

"Maybe."

"If you won't agree, then I'll have to talk to Levi and Nina."

"Fuck that."

Tucker glowered at Mason. "Don't even pull your shit with me. We're all in this equally. You are not the man in charge."

"I'm the one who's been keeping our shit together for years. Don't get me wrong, Tuck. I'm thrilled you've made so much progress in your life.

No one deserves it more. But I've worked my ass off making sure no detail fell through the cracks when it came to our lives and the welfare of *everyone* involved. Do you have any idea what that entails?"

He did. More than Mason knew. Unfortunately the best-kept secrets were still secrets and one day they would explode.

"Have you heard anything more from that reporter?"

Mason's eyes darkened and a scowl crossed his face. "She's still here and nosing around."

Tucker took a moment to study his friend's body language. Eyebrows pulled together, arms crossed over his chest, and narrowed eyes. Interesting. "Anything to worry about yet?" He hated the idea of the news media ruining the fragile peace they had. It was bad enough he'd have to burden Maggie…

"I'm going to have to talk to her. The more she pokes the better likelihood she'll find something by accident."

"Maybe it's time for a contingency plan."

"If you've got an idea that doesn't include an orange jumpsuit for the three of us, I'm all ears."

He didn't. It wasn't as if he hadn't run every fucking possible scenario through his head a thousand times over the years. None of them were good. "I think it's time we talk to Levi. I've got a bad feeling about all this. Too much is happening all at once."

"Yeah, well—"

That did not sound good. "What?" Here it came, the other shoe.

"Levi's gone missing."

"Excuse me?"

"I'm certain I don't need to repeat myself."

"God dammit, Mason. Stop with the macho bullshit. I am not above beating the ever living crap out of you."

A sardonic smile crossed Mason's face. "I'd love to see you try."

He narrowed his eyes in warning. "Tell me about Levi. How do you know he's missing?"

"Because I've been looking for him for three weeks."

"That's why you came back here. This isn't about the reporter at all."

Mason's silence damned him. "Look, don't get crazy. The reporter thing is real, but yes, part of what drove me back here was the hope that I'd find Levi back in his hometown."

Not one to panic, Tucker straightened in his seat and started formulating a plan. "What do you know?"

"It looks like he went off the grid about a month ago. As far as the investigator I hired can tell, he packed a bag, closed his house up and hit the road."

Tucker relaxed a fraction. "So he went on vacation?"

"Maybe. Wherever he went, he didn't want anyone to know. He's not used any of his credit cards or his cell phone."

"I don't like this. Things have been quiet for years and now it's pure chaos. You get the impression things are unraveling?"

"I'm sure Levi will show up sooner or later."

"It's not just Levi, I'm worried about. Things are changing and if we don't change with them this isn't going to end well."

Mason stood, pulled out his wallet and laid down some cash for the drinks he'd consumed. "For our sake I hope you're wrong."

Tucker sat silent watching his college friend leave. Like it or not their lives and everything around them was evolving. The time had come for some changes.

First, he'd start with Maggie.

Ready for more?

Be sure to pick up the next in the series, **Levi's Ultimatum**, available now.

About the Author

Eliza Gayle lives a life full of sexy shapeshifters, blood boiling vamps and a dark desire for bondage…until she steps away from her computer and has to tend to her family.

She graduated Magna Cum Laude (which her husband translated into something very naughty) from college with a dual degree in Human Resource Management and Sociology. That education, a love of the metaphysical and a dirty mind comes in handy when she sits down to create new characters and worlds. The trick is getting her to sit still.

…Join her in her world. The door is always open and the next red-hot adventure is just a page away.

Look for Eliza on the Web at http://www.emgayle.com or check out her blog at http://www.emgayle.com/blog.
She is also on Facebook at http://www.facebook.com/AuthorEMGayle and Twitter at http://www.twitter.com/authoremgayle

Continue reading for a delicious sneak peek!

Afterword

Thank you so much for reading *Tucker's Fall*, the first in my Purgatory Masters series. I hope you enjoyed reading it as much as I loved writing it. I'm hard at work on my next romance, but don't despair, I have several other books available to tide you over.

The Purgatory Club holds a special place in my heart because it's based on a fetish show I used to attend when I lived in Charlotte, North Carolina. A while back I began writing novellas that focused on the club and different fetishes that could be explored there. Those stories are all available now. If you've not read them, I suggest you start with *Roped*. There you'll discover many of the characters you saw in *Tucker's Fall*.

Welcome to Purgatory! A club for every desire...

Katie has a fetish for rope and she's had her eye on riggers Leo and Quinn for quite some time. Week after week she goes to the club and watches them tie up women from afar, while she imagines their rough rope against her own skin.

Now the two hunky men have decided to make their move. But is plus-sized Katie ready to turn her fantasies into reality?

Excerpt:

Quinn grasped Katie's wrist and flipped her around to face him. His amber eyes pierced through her with a heated intensity as he watched her reactions. "You come here week after week and stand here looking down at us as we work. Do you think we don't notice the longing on your face? The way your body squirms as we wrap more and more rope around the girls who ask us to? Why are you torturing yourself? Or should I say…what are you waiting for?"

She closed her eyes to his questions, searching for an adequate answer when she knew there was none. How could she deny the truth? "I admire your work. What's wrong with that?"

His fingers gently grasped her chin and raised her head back up, forcing her to look at him. "We see you, Katie, we know what you need. Why do you hide here?"

She bristled against his words, shame heating her face. "I'm not hiding, Quinn, I'm just observing. I'm here and I'm alone, yet no one ever approaches or speaks to me. Which is fine, but don't tell me that I'm hiding. What am I supposed to do? Throw myself at someone?"

A grin split Quinn's handsome face, revealing the beautiful smile she loved so much. She always noticed how happy his job made him and she envied him that feeling. Some ties were more intense than others as evidenced by the hard lines of his face when he concentrated or the occasional bulge in his pants when a willing female turned him on. It was those moments when she had fleeting thoughts of both him and Leo taking her for their own. The popular riggers were frequently gossiped about around Purgatory, and word was they had a great time playing the scene together but hadn't taken a submissive of their own for a very long time.

"You don't have to get defensive with me, babe. I'm not sure what's wrong with the men in this club, letting you spend all your time alone. Their loss is my gain, though." He leaned closer, his lips a breath away from her own. The sharp tang of citrus filled her nostrils and she imagined he'd just come from a break where he would have eaten an orange. Did he realize even the way his hands peeled the skin from an orange could turn a woman inside out?

Katie sucked in a slow breath, afraid to move. She worried he would kiss her as much as she worried that he wouldn't. She was in a mood tonight, and watching the play stations hadn't helped but instead stoked the flames inside her until, now pressed against one of the men of her nightly dreams, she wanted nothing more than to submit to his every whim. She ached with the desire to be touched, to be tied, and to be fucked by Quinn and Leo.

He edged a little closer, but instead of kissing her like she expected, he stroked her lips with his tongue. A gentle touch that was more like a taste than a kiss. He leaned into her until they were pressed together from hips to breast, and his erection was unmistakable pushed against her belly and pelvis. His hot tongue licked at the corner of her mouth and along the seam of her lips. She opened farther on a soft sigh but he only continued his exploration.

Her own arousal went off the charts as she

rolled her hips against his. A low growl sounded in his throat and he pulled his head back from hers. "Careful, Katie. For a girl who professes to being happy alone, your body is quickly making a liar out of you."

She clamped her mouth shut and tried to pull back, but there was nowhere to go. He had her against the railing and his arms still held her in place. "I think we should stop this, people are starting to stare."